IN THE BEGINNING

"Six weeks ago . . . we lost two Seers." Radis looked from Tyrees to Bolla, eyes wide. "I just thought it a—a sad coincidence at the time."

Tyrees's eyes glinted their deadly blue. In spite of the circumstances, Radis and Bolla took note of the sudden change in him.

"How? How, Radis?"

"Well, if I remember accurately . . . Pegasus system . . . Retor-quel—one of the new Seers. Autopsy says 'cerebral aneurysm.'" Radis looked at Tyrees in time to see thin lips draw tighter over his teeth.

"Four days later—Pren-spel. Same system . . ."

"I remember him," said Tyrees very softly.

"One hundred thirty-two standard years—old even for a Tercian. 'Viral infection—respiratory.' Very quick."

Radis had nothing more to say. He looked at Tyrees and knew. He *knew.*

Tyrees's fist came crashing down on the chair arm. "You should have realized, Radis. You should have told me."

"Wait now, you two!" sputtered Bolla. "Just what *is* going on here?"

Tyrees rose slowly and walked to the balcony window.

"Murder," he said.

ROBERT O'RIORDAN

CADRE MESSIAH

ACE BOOKS, NEW YORK

To my father

This book is an Ace original edition, and has never been previously published.

CADRE MESSIAH

An Ace Book / published by arrangement with the author

PRINTING HISTORY
Ace edition / November 1988

ISBN: 0-441-09016-8

Ace Books are published by The Berkley Publishing Group,
200 Madison Avenue, New York, New York 10016.
The name "ACE" and the "A" logo
are trademarks belonging to Charter Communications, Inc.
PRINTED IN THE UNITED STATES OF AMERICA

10 9 8 7 6 5 4 3 2 1

One

TYREES STOOD ON the balcony of the Citadel, looking up at the night sky, but it was not the cold pricks of starlight that drew his eyes, or his thoughts. It was the ocean of blackness surrounding them. The stars were distant, but the Void reached down with black claws that penetrated to his soul.

He looked with loathing upon its potent indifference, like a widowed fisherwoman looks upon the sea.

Yet it drew him. The absence of color, the absence of form, the absence of life, drew him as a black hole draws with its voracious nullity. It wanted to swallow him, but was infinitely patient; he wanted to swallow *it,* but he was not.

He thought of his grandfather, and an old hurt nudged from inside. Somehow, though, even murder was acceptable. An evil, but human choice had been made, and a dark hand had struck. When he thought of Meta-sol, his spiritual father, the pain was shot with rage. His Mentor had died because he was old—and because he had fought death so hard.

Pol Tyrees, Pol-Nesol-Rast, *Vitar,* raised a puny white fist to the blackness and shook it with full awareness that his fury was ridiculous. Vitar. Life-giver. The title bestowed by a galaxy upon its reluctant god. Ironically, he could not hear that word without tasting acid beneath his tongue. He brought the fist down and turned to walk slowly from the balcony. He felt foolish anger, like a small boy derided with laughter by the neighborhood bully.

The entire top floor of the Citadel was reserved for his personal use—more for security reasons than by preference, for his needs were simple—and he made use of few of the rooms. Two years earlier the building had housed the offices of the Council of the Regnum—the group of men and women who had become the sham symbol of galactic democracy, the plaything of their megalomaniacal Chairman. Now, the Chairman was an inmate of a high-security asylum for the incurably insane. He was still given to nakedness, shredding his clothing into tiny patches with his teeth, when he could.

Tyrees paced restlessly. He turned on lights in rooms only to stare at walls for a moment and leave them. By the standards of what was luxurious—on any world, let alone Regnum, the seat of galactic government for over a thousand years—these rooms were Spartan. Nothing in them was without function. But what he looked for, he did not find. Visitors (the fingers of a hand outnumbered these) always took note of the absence of decor, but none realized that something so ordinarily ubiquitous as a mirror was also missing.

His pacing was suddenly brought to a startled halt by a smeared reflection of himself in the huge balcony window. He leaned one way, then the other. The image shimmered in and out of focus. The black nightdrop behind the glass refused to speak clearly. Only a shrouded, ghostly figure of a man was given back, but enough to reveal that the head was totally without hair and that the eyes flared with extraordinary intensity. Finally, he snorted, and whirled to fall into the nearest chair. The fiery blue eyes went to the ceiling, casting. The face was old, not with the soft folds and mottled skin fashioned slowly by years, but with the lines and hollows of time compressed by the fist of experience. The hands spoke for the body, and they were young—the hands of a slender athlete.

Tyrees let a long sigh empty his lungs; his eyes fell from above and closed. In seconds a transformation took place that even the most accomplished of actors could not imitate: every muscle of his body released its tension, every fiber loosed. The lines of pain—like those of a migrane victim—disappeared from his forehead. He seemed to sleep. Magically, Tyrees became inanimate, a finely wrought wax figure into which its creator had been able to craft every minutiae of life except motion; since eyes were beyond even his art, he left them closed.

A pleasant hum sounded. The eyes opened. Unlike the utterly still body, they were exactly as they had been—banked blue embers. A moment passed before his hand moved to touch a square of dull light in the chair arm, and the hiss of a sliding door could be heard from an anteroom. The voices followed it.

"Radis, your problem is that you don't get to hear this often enough lately—you're an idiot!"

"Dr. Bolla! Please!" Unoffended laughter. "Where is that professorial objectivity you usually display?"

As they entered the room and saw Tyrees, their attitudes leavened. They paused and simply stood for a moment, unobtrusively but unabashedly looking him over. They always watched him carefully, and over the last year they had felt reason to be encouraged. He had not regained his hair, of course, but the emaciated hollowness had left his face, the pale translucence his skin. Some muscle bulk had returned to his body. For a time, particularly just before their coup, his flesh had come to exude that grand ascetic denial, as if life itself were an ether too alien to breathe.

Tyrees's voice was soft, calm, resonantly magnetic.

"Hans. Radis. You both look well. And still quibbling, as you were when you left a month ago. Sit down, will you? Radis, the cape becomes you more than ever."

Radis smiled somewhat sheepishly, but the gestures that maneuvered the long, black cape as he sat in a chair were as natural as those of a settling bird.

"Thank you, Vitar"—Tyrees blinked—"but I did have one of these things on my shoulders most of my life. As you did."

"Radis, how many times have you promised not to call me that?"

"Sorry, uh . . . forgot again. It's just that . . . well, that's how I think of you." Radis shrugged powerful shoulders. To escape the blue eyes he undid his collar clasp, letting the cape fall to the back of his chair.

Tyrees snorted. "You, you and the doctor here—of all people—should know better."

Another snort, this more derisive, came from Dr. Hans Bolla. He was still shifting his pendulous girth in the chair, like a whale settling to the bottom. "Come come come, Pol. Let the man call you by the name that several billion others do." He chuckled, and the lowest chin jiggled on his chest. "*I* call you Pol because a man who gets to be as old as I am has earned the right to be sacrilegious."

Tyrees turned his head to look out at the night through the balcony window. His voice became even softer. Of all men, only the two now listening were capable of detecting the almost invisible filament of anxiety wound through it—Radis more than Bolla, because of his training under the Seers.

"Yes. They think me a god. I'd rather you laughed at me like the doctor, Radis." Radis pursed his lips, eyes cast down, but said nothing.

Bolla rubbed his bald pate and spoke in the tones of feigned ingenuousness. "I remember a time when you might have thought your title perfectly appropriate, Pol." He also remembered how afraid he was, for he was fully convinced even then that the man he addressed was capable of more—for good or evil—than any man ever born.

Tyrees nodded minutely. "Perhaps . . . but that time is past."

Bolla prodded. "You find omniscience somewhat trying now, do you?" The head twitched slightly and the blue eyes flared. Bolla's fear flared with them. "I'm sorry, Pol," he sighed.

"Unkind cut. I know you've changed . . . but . . . but I guess I don't like this version either. I'm worried about you."

Tyrees looked at him for a long time, long enough for the old, obese psychologist to squirm inside. Nevertheless, the bulging and sagging exterior could summon a strength that some had reason to know was there. He summoned it now, for this was perilous ground indeed. Tyrees never, *never* discussed deep, personal feelings. But damn it, he had pinched the cheek of this . . . this *god* when he was five years old!

"There is nothing to worry about, Doctor," said Tyrees finally. It was the same, infinitely controlled and compelling voice. A Svengali voice. "We have more important matters to talk about."

"No. Nothing is more important than this, Pol. Nothing. For a change, you're going to listen."

Radis had been staring his surprise at Bolla. But now he interrupted. "Yes. Yes, I agree. The Regnum can wait for a bit. I have something to say too."

Tyrees's eyebrows arched. He seemed genuinely amused, though there was no smile. " 'The Regnum can wait'? A galactic civilization on the brink of chaos can wait while two amateur psychologists—forgive me, Hans—one *real* psychologist, and a Security Cadre officer, hammer the dents out of their leader's warped mind?"

"Don't ridicule us, Pol," said Bolla. "We're concerned."

"Oh?"

"Yes, I—"

"Please, Doctor," said Radis, interrupting again. "I don't know what you're going to say, but I want to get something out of the way first." He turned to Tyrees. There was a quiver in his lips that belied the uniform and the bearing of command in the muscular body. "I call you Vitar. *Life-Giver*. You saved my life when no man ever born could. As the doctor said, millions call you that, and not *one* of them has more right than I. Not one. I don't know *what* you are, okay? But to me, you are Vitar." Radis seemed satisfied with this, for he nodded to himself, without looking for a reaction from Tyrees. Then he looked to

Bolla. "Your turn, Doctor."

Bolla, always a loquacious man who could change language register at will, whether it be that of a street-tough or a dinner speaker, now hesitated. Feeling the force of the distant blue eyes like a sea feels the moon, he finally settled upon the psychologist's ultimate weapon, a devastating secret held close by the first shaman and the last for the eleventh hour when everything hung in the balance—the purity of truth, delivered with the purest form language could muster.

"Pol," he said, "listen to me, please." His voice was husky. "You want to talk about the Regnum. You want . . . like a good physician, to restore her to health. That is a noble sentiment, Pol, and Radis, and I . . . well, we share it. But *you yourself* are not healthy. . . . No!" Bolla held up a hand when he saw Tyrees about to object. "Listen to me. Accept some facts. The Regnum is now divided into three balanced factions. One—the majority now—is the manifestation of your will, the New Covenant. They want the freedom to pursue individual growth according to the teachings of *The Teraac*." Here, Bolla paused. Stubby fingers massaged the back of his neck. "I wish . . . I wish I were younger, though that's a poor excuse. I would have begun the Learning myself, like Radis. But . . . never mind. The second faction, and still the most politically powerful, is our inheritance from the old regime. They want their toys back, and they want vengeance, Pol. We plucked the reigns from their hands more through surprise than defeat, so only their most demonstrably corrupt leaders have been removed, and the infrastructure is still there."

"I know all this, Doctor." No impatience was revealed in the tone, but Tyrees rose from his chair and moved to the balcony window. He spoke with his back to them. "We usually criticize you for those vast, unholy theories of yours—talking about the galactic civilization like a cage of guinea pigs. Now, you dwell on the obvious."

Bolla grabbed both arms of his chair and pulled himself forward. "I'm starting with what you will accept, damn it. And in a moment I'll be getting to *you*." When Tyrees did not respond, Bolla settled back, disappointed. The timbres of pleading sincerity left his voice and he went on in his most professorial manner. "The third faction is always present in the mass human dynamic—relatively predictable, but dangerous and never to be ignored. I refer, of course, to the self-servers, those without commitment except to their own well being—in short, the vultures. They will wait for the flow of blood before they strike.

"And now, Pol-Nesol-Rast, Seer of the Gathering . . . *Vitar,* I come to you."

Still Tyrees did not respond, but he turned from the window to face Bolla. The simple black tunic that he always wore—a stylized space technic's coverall, really—together with the ink of the night sky behind him, threw the pale skin of his hairless head into stark relief. The tunic had come to be his badge of office, though Bolla secretly believed it to be an unconscious imitation of the Cadre uniform—capeless, but very like that Radis wore, minus the high collar. It was a throwback to the days when Tyrees wore it with total conviction as a Cadre One, when he served as a guardian of the galactic empire he now ruled.

Bolla cringed invisibly as Tyrees stared at him, a statue of dark rock. He was always unnerved by the man when he was not moving. His stillness was utter, like death. Bolla drew a breath and plunged out onto the ice cast by the blue eyes.

"There's something wrong with you, Pol. You're not functioning properly. You . . . you're unhappy." Bolla himself was unhappy with his choice of that vague and "unprofessional" word, but he was encouraged because it produced some animation in the face—a slow, sad smile.

"I am grateful for your concern, Hans, but happiness is something I've never sought. I don't know what it is. Do you?"

"No," sighed Bolla. "Nevertheless, we *all* seek it. You have always been a man of . . . of remoteness, but lately you've become even more detached. You've sacrificed a great deal to stand where you are now, yet all I see is indifference. And we need your help! Radis and I had to badger you for this meeting—the first in a month! You seem more and more alone . . . unconcerned. . . .''

"Sacrifices?" Tyrees's word cut into Bolla's like a knife. It was keened with understated bitterness. "Yes, there have been sacrifices. Many. The count depends on how far back you want to go. I tend to start with Dace Sestus, almost thirty years ago. I was a Cadre Two then, and he was my only friend. I killed him.''

A startled Radis sent a quizzical look at Bolla. The doctor was shaking his head. "I know about Ses, Pol, but you're not making sense. You killed him in the line of duty. He attacked you. And what has he got to do with—''

"He had no options. The Cadre would have court-martialed and executed him after I arrested him for passing information. A civilian would have been slapped on the wrist—but he was Cadre.''

Bolla was confused and irritated. "Yes, that's the sort of thing that eventually turned you against the system. I understand that. Unfortunate, but—''

"My first *sacrifice*," cut in Tyrees once more. "Someone who didn't have to die." He turned to the window again and spoke to the darkness. "Then there was my grandfather. You have his title now, Radis—Cadre Proctor. Murdered by the Chairman. Another *sacrifice*, and I'm not even up to your time yet, am I?''

His listeners were now deeply disturbed. Bolla, especially, had only wanted to nudge Tyrees into even the most tacit admission that he was troubled. That would have been more than he had hoped for. But this was a virtual outpouring for Tyrees, and its morbid coloring frightened him. He glanced aside and saw some of that fear mirrored in Radis's face. Quickly he raised his hand to caution silence before turning his attention back to Tyrees. Bolla could see only his back and a pale, blurred reflection of his disembodied face in the plasteel glass. The lips of the face were moving, as if the words were coming from them, as if they were speaking to Tyrees himself, quietly, venomously.

"And we can't leave out your friend, Councilman Leeth, Doctor, who came with you to warn me on Tercet. Atomized . . . along with a whole space crew. Molecules of human flesh spread through parsecs of space . . . And then there was Spel-sol and members of *our* space crew . . ." His voice began to lose volume, slowing like a dying wind. "And Meta-sol . . . Meta-sol. Nothing could justify the sacrifice of Meta-sol." The sounds of the words from the face in the glass had now fallen to soft hisses. Its lips paused, still open, then whispered two more words.

"And Shaamlik."

Bolla wanted to scream at the face—what, he didn't know. Instead, with careful calm, he said, "You know Shaamlik's still alive, Pol." As if he hadn't spoken, two more, almost inaudible puffs of sound came from the image on the glass.

"And me."

Two

Yes, the darkness is rich indeed, at its heart. But there, too, lies its greatest peril—and there can be no compromise. Man was born to fight to the light. It is a curse, perhaps, but we must possess the strength—or we would not have been born at all.

—The Sayings of Meta-sol

TYREES STOOD MOTIONLESS over the head of the bed. Bolla and Radis kept their distance, remaining near the doorway, as if to come nearer would be to commit some unspeakable breach of sensitivity.

It was the first time they had seen Shaamlik since just after the coup. She looked now just as she did then—an unmoving form on the bed, a still, tragic figure oblivious to the still, tragic figures below her on the floor. Bolla had gently pulled Tyrees's arms away from Meta-sol. Radis had carried the child-light body of the old Tercian away. Tyrees stayed where he was, kneeling, for a long time. Bolla remembered well his expression; it went beyond grief and into some realm of infinite fatigue where motion was travesty. He remembered, too, Meta-sol's cane stretched on the bed alongside Shaamlik.

Yes, she looked the same. Her face would *always* look the same, for it was literally a mask. The flash fire aboard *Condor* had, like the passing of an evil hand, wiped away the flesh above her neck, wiped away, too, her sanity. The polymer mask that

10

saved her life was perfect, grotesquely beautiful: there was an almost invisible line which would allow the jaw to move; there were the smooth convexes of the kind fashioned by sculptors who knew that stone could not be chiseled into eyes; there were discreet perforations among the subtle, stylized formations of ears and nose and mouth. The thin coverlet rose and fell along the curves of a woman's body, which was still beautiful, if somewhat wasted, and hid the passage of tubing that brought, and kept, her life.

Tyrees leaned over, but did not touch her.

"You see?" he said finally. "You are right, Doctor. She's not dead. She's worse than dead."

Bolla loathed the notion of being drawn into this morass of hopelessness, and he suspected that Tyrees's troubled mind found its blight in sources even beyond the catatonia of a woman he once loved.

"She is physiologically sound, Pol. Perhaps in time—"

"In time we will all be compost," said Tyrees quietly.

The sight of Shaamlik touched Radis deeply, because it forced him to think of himself, near death, almost four years earlier. An inoperable brain tumor was eating him up, slowly, until Tyrees and Meta-sol—at great risk to their own lives—went "in" and excised it. That was the beginning of the name, Vitar. To the devout of the New Covenant it might have been metaphorical. To him it was real.

"Vitar," he said. He ignored Tyrees's look. "Has she not spoken at all? Has she not moved in all this time?"

Tyrees hesitated, then frowned. "I . . . I'm not sure. I thought she spoke . . . my name. I thought she moved her arm and touched me." His fingers found a spot on the back of his neck. "Just after I found Meta-sol . . . I was on the floor with my back to her. . . ." He banished the thought with a vicious shake of his head. "No. I was in shock, I suppose. Exhausted. Irrational."

"But did you try—"

"I tried," said Tyrees harshly. "Long before that night. She is insane, Radis. *Mad.*"

"But—"

"It was like walking into a storm of fire. You cannot imagine it."

"Will you let me try?" Radis knew his words would sound presumptuous, and he was more than a little afraid, but there was no limit to what he owed this man. "I'm much more adept now, perhaps more than you realize."

Some of the blue flint in Tyrees's eyes softened as he looked at Radis. "More adept than Meta-sol?" he asked.

Radis frowned. "Well, no, of course not."

"Why do you think he died?" Radis looked uncertainly at Bolla, who tongued his lips and looked at the floor. "You are both wrong. You *think* he died because he followed me off the time track when we ousted the Chairman—correct? You saw the effect it had on me, and you thought it was just too much for him."

"I should have known," said Bolla, speaking for the first time since entering the room. He looked at Radis. "I don't think you saw the cane."

"He died in there," said Tyrees, looking at the perfect, inhuman face below him. His words were clear shards of ice. "He was trying to help her for me. Another *sacrifice*. A thousand Seers, a thousand *Vitars* will never replace him. . . . A colossal waste."

"*He* wouldn't think that way, Pol," said Bolla quietly.

"Perhaps not." Tyrees did not lift his eyes from the mask. "But if it were going to be anyone—it should have been me."

For a time there was silence. The lighting of the room was subdued, glowing dully off the higher planes of the hard mask. Radis looked desperately at Bolla, who shook his head as he sought for words.

"Pol . . . that is misplaced guilt. Unhealthy, dangerous guilt. You should know better."

Finally Tyrees's eyes rose from the mask. He smiled.

"Ah, but I do, Doctor. I do." He began to move away from the bed. "Come. We've wasted enough . . . *time*, haven't we? Let's get back to business."

"Wait . . . please." Radis held both hands up, palms forward. "Please, answer a question for me?" He was a large man, powerful and imposing, a man born and trained to command; yet at this moment he was a small boy begging adult secrets from his father. Tyrees nodded.

"I spent a great deal of time with Meta-sol, almost as much as you, Vitar. He told me how . . . different you and he were. Tell me if I understand. He was amazed, *stunned* by your power. You were . . . 'like a water-demon,' he said. 'An irresistible torrent of water.' But he had . . . finesse? You were power and he was finesse?"

Tyrees smiled again, but ruefully.

"If you had to put it into words—and you can't—I suppose I wouldn't object to those. Yes, we were different. Neither of us, alone, could have helped *you*, for example."

"Well then," said Radis, now excited. "Maybe together, you and I—"

"Forget it." Tyrees walked by them, heading back to the balcony room and forcing them to hurry after. Bolla grunted irritably with the effort of keeping up, his stubby legs taking two strides to their one. He wouldn't have made the effort, except that Tyrees was speaking as he went.

"You don't understand, Radis, so I'll put it bluntly, and that will be the end of it—you don't know enough. Meta-sol may have been able to make a guess as to your potential, but I can't. I'm only sure of this: if you opened yourself up to Shaamlik now, your brain would be *fried*. You'd be dead or a zombie—take your pick." As they entered the windowed room again, he turned to Radis, driving home his words. "Whatever it has become out there"—he motioned sideways with his head, the gesture taking in several hundred worlds and billions of people—"the New Covenant is *not* some . . . some mystical toy for little boys to play with for their amusement. Nor is it some sentimental, religious pap that promises Nirvana!"

By this time Tyrees's eyes were ablaze with some undefined anger. Bolla, particularly, was frightened by it, for even he—by choice not an adept—could feel the very air change, become infused with a charge that nubbed at the hair on the backs of his hands. For many years now, with the best of motives, he thought, he had been trying to pull Tyrees out of himself into a greater awareness of his own humanity, into a recognition and acceptance of his *fallibility*. This night, with Tyrees's uncharacteristic openness, his display of anger and uncertainties, Bolla was afraid of precisely that. This man held a galaxy in the palm of his hand. Perhaps that was why he was finally bending under the weight of it. . . .

Tyrees was now back in his chair, glaring at Radis, who, though crestfallen and subdued, was hanging on his words.

"The New Covenant, Radis, is quite simply, self-discipline —the marriage of mind and body, and the control of both. Call it self-knowledge if you like. It takes a great deal of single-minded effort. There is no room for anything else."

Suddenly Tyrees was on his feet again, pointing his finger at Radis like an accusing father. The action was so swift that it was registered only as an after-image on the backs of Bolla's eyes.

"Can you pull your intestines up into your chest cavity?"

Radis blinked. "No, Vitar," he said softly.

"Then you have things to learn yet. Then you will begin to have some control over your immediate environment. Then, perhaps," said Tyrees, turning slowly now back to his window and the darkness beyond it, "you will know how little it is you can really accomplish."

"The time track," murmured Radis. "You're talking about the time track, aren't you?"

Tyrees did not answer. Instead he reached out strangely, with one hand palm forward, until it was stopped by the glass. It rested there for a long moment before the fingers pulled away, curled into knuckles, and gently struck the hard, invisible barrier. Tap. Tap. Tap.

"Vitar?"

No response. Bolla saw the white face in the window again, now with a fist under it. Tap. Tap. Tap. He could have been tapping out a secret code at a door he was loath to enter.

"Pol, shall we get back to business?"

Bolla strode to his chair and sat without invitation. Tyrees turned to them with an abstracted air, but nodded slowly. When they were all seated once more, he seemed more himself.

"Your analysis, Doctor—the three factions. Were you finished? Any recommendations?"

"Yes, but they'll keep for the moment. I want to hear *your* views first."

Tyrees shrugged. "Our policy to date has been simple—consolidation. I see no reason to change that course, especially if the New Covenant continues to grow. Then all we need is . . . time. Agreed?"

Bolla sat humpty-dumpty fashion with his legs spread far apart, the knees almost unbent. His main function in the new regime was shepherding the Council, with which Radis also sat as the Cadre Proctor. Like the former Chairman, they dictated policy, and made no bones about it. Within the lines drawn by that policy, however, the Council members made the decisions by vote, a resurrected practice that had surprised and pleased them. Bolla loathed politics and made an unhappy dictator. He had long since come to two conclusions: that he was best suited to the academic life as a probability theorist, which he had left many years earlier; and that he would never again resume it. He stretched his jaw out and up, pushing his younger face to the surface for a moment out of the accumulated folds.

"What do you think, Radis? Just hang tight? Let the tide of the New Covenant gradually wash over the old order, huh?"

The pinched lines between Radis's eyes showed that he was still preoccupied with Tyrees, but they disappeared as he brought himself to the matter at hand.

"Uh, well, at least the Cadre is solid now. It's been easier than I anticipated, in fact, but I should have known from the first. For centuries it's been loyal to one idea—a unified and peaceful galactic order called the Regnum. Politicos come and go, you know? And the Chairman had eroded that idea more than most, causing a lot of resentment because the Cadre was used more and more as a political tool." He grinned at Tyrees. "As a matter of fact, Vitar, I've come to realize just how compatible the Cadre and the New Covenant are. Regimen. Targeted goals. Dedication. Self-discipline. The Cadre was our training ground for the Seers!"

Tyrees nodded and said, "Yes, I suppose it was—in a way. The Cadre fashions a tough mind, in any case. The Seers have to have *that* to start with."

"Ahem." Bolla clasped hands and made a childish display of twiddling his thumbs with mock impatience. "I realize that being gentlemen of leisure, you two can while away the time with pleasant reminiscences—but I'm a busy man, and a much older one. I take it neither of you has any serious concerns about the current state of affairs?"

Radis scowled. "Okay, Doctor. You can dump it now. You've been itching ever since we got here."

"I've just been waiting to see if one of you would identify a rather obvious problem. I've been disappointed."

"Bullshit," said Radis, laughing. "I know you've been tinkering with Anavex again. 'Obvious,' huh? What does your kinky little machine tell us we should start worrying about three millenia from now?"

"As you well know, it's a *program,* not a machine," sniffed Bolla, aware that he was being teased but feeling hurt nevertheless. Anavex was his brainchild, a probability program ten years in the making, which was capable of predicting behavioral trends on the galactic level. It fed upon sociological and psychological data on such a massive scale that, to acquire such data and the hardware to process it, he had gone to Tyrees's grandfather for help. He got what he wanted, but from that point on his work was classified, and he had stepped naively out of the cozy nest of academia and into the bloodred maw of politics.

Radis was still chuckling. "So I was right—Anavex has coughed up more prophecy! What does the ol' crystal ball have to say, Doctor?"

"There was a time," said Bolla, fixing him with a stare that he had once reserved for recalcitrant graduates, "when even the Chairman called Anavex 'the Oracle.' Not too far from your crystal ball, is it?—except that he knew better than to deride it, as you do."

Radis sobered. "Sorry, Doctor. I mean no disrespect, of course." He hesitated briefly. "It's just that I'm a practical man, and Anavex always looks *too* far ahead. It seems to ignore immediate problems. For example, it didn't help the Chairman much, did it? He still had the beast after you jumped ship."

"No, and thank the Maker," sighed Bolla. "I see you still don't understand it." He struggled with a stubby arm, reaching behind him to massage his lower back. "In the first place, the Chairman didn't have *me* to run it for him—Anavex isn't a family-budgeting program, you know. Besides, bringing in a probability predictor is one thing—antitemporating is quite another." Bolla steepled his fingers and waited smugly for the question. Radis couldn't resist obliging.

"'Antitemporating'?"

"Yes—my own term. Working backward in time from a probable future. Fixing trend precipitators—causal factors, if you will. You see, once 'trend fulmination' is reached—or that point of no return after which Anavex feels its predicted trend *must* come about—there are still a number of different vectors that may end the same way."

Radis squinted up the barrel of an imaginary gun aimed by his own hand. "I asked for this, didn't I? All right, Doctor, I surrender. What the hell does that jargon *mean?*"

Bolla smiled seraphically. "It means, young man, that though the Citadel has only one exit, there are dozens of different ways of getting to it."

"Ah . . . thank you. Then 'antitemporizing' sorts the different ways out?"

"Correct."

To this point Tyrees had only been listening, though even that term had a relative value when applied to him. An observer never knew the level of his attention at any given time. Light flickered off his skull as he turned to Bolla.

"So, we have finally come to the point of this meeting, Hans?"

"Yes. Radis and I—we have followed your instructions, Pol. No more 'routine' meetings, you said. Only matters of 'crisis or policy,' you said. Well, this comes under the second category." Bolla paused for effect, for he loved, as all teachers do, the drama of revelation. "You will be gratified to learn that the phenomenon we refer to as the New Covenant has reached trend fulmination."

"That's nice," said Radis, unimpressed. "But hardly surprising. We've been working toward it long enough. That means that Anavex confirms the New Covenant as the dominant movement in the Regnum for a long time to come?"

"Correct again, my boy. Actually, that point was reached over a year ago, shortly after the coup."

"Then you've merely confirmed. All our policy is—"

"He's not finished, Radis." Tyrees's voice had not risen in volume, but its timbre had changed, truncating Radis's sentence like a laser slicing a tree trunk. "Please get to the point, Doctor."

Bolla scowled. He had intended to milk his drama slowly. "Very well. My antitemporations, gentlemen. There are many vectors, many different scenarios that allow the supremacy of the New Covenant." He hesitated again, this time because he found himself reluctant to go on.

Tyrees granted him a single word as a prompt. "Oh?"

Bolla licked his lips. "The most disturbing facet of my calculations is your leadership, Pol. It occupies only *one* vector. One. That is . . . astonishing."

Tyrees's head moved slightly, but there was no other sign of surprise. Radis felt his jaw open absurdly and remain there. He struggled to fill the hole left by his incredulity.

"That's ridiculous, Doctor," he said. "Something is wrong!"

"Not with Anavex," returned Bolla quietly. "It doesn't make mistakes like that, nor do I. You see—"

"It doesn't matter." There was nothing in Tyrees's voice but acceptance—and a suggestion of relief. "If the New Covenant prevails, it doesn't matter."

Bolla struggled to his feet, something he never did out of restlessness or pique. Usually when he rose from a sitting position it was to go somewhere. This time he shifted around his chair, patting it with a palm, nudging it with a toe, flicking it with abstract fingers as if it were a strange artifact. Finally he hiked his voluminous robe and thumped off to one side.

"It does matter," he said. "It matters very much. We do not know what forms the New Covenant can take." He looked intently at Tyrees. "It is a . . . an enlightened concept, and I think it shows man the destiny he was meant from the beginning to fulfill. But it still has no sanctity beyond that of its believers, beyond the will of its *leaders*. It can be *used*, as easily as the Chairman used the old political order."

Tyrees frowned. "But we have no indication of anything insidious."

"None that we can *see*, perhaps. And there is something else, gentlemen. Just as disturbing." Here Bolla shambled back to his chair, letting himself into it with all the attention that age and obesity called for. "Most vectors do not even show evidence of the *Seers*."

Radis hit his chair arm with an angry slap. "Now, come *on*, Doctor. That's impossible! They're not just—just bloody priests! The Seers are *teachers—trainers*. There is no *progress* without them, no learning! Take the Seers away and there is no New Covenant!"

Bolla met Radis's anger with a mild stare. "No New Covenant as you—or your Vitar—conceive of it. It is, after all, a basically passive, inherently contemplative movement. It is apolitical, and spurns materialism; it is insular, absorbed with the *individual* human self. In short, it is vulnerable. It can be manipulated, jaded by other interests, especially if the Seers are somehow eliminated, and then—''

"Wait!" Radis had a hand up. He had gone milk pale. "Six weeks ago—no, seven, at least—we lost two Seers." He looked from one to the other, eyes wide. "I just thought it a—a sad coincidence at the time. Could it be more?''

Bolla leaned forward, jowls quivering. "Two Seers died?''

"Yes. In the same system, a few days apart. One was an original, a Tercian.''

Tyrees's eyes glinted their deadly blue. In spite of the circumstances, Radis and Bolla took note of the sudden change in him. Without any real animation evident, he was suddenly more charged with purpose than they had seen him in months.

"How? How, Radis?''

"Well, if I remember accurately . . .'' When Radis hesitated, Tyrees slapped a square of dull light in his chair arm. A section of wall to their left slid away to reveal a large screen, already glowing softly. The low table between them came to life, too, its glossly black surface losing its opacity to a set of embedded touch pads. Tyrees kicked the table almost violently, sending it across to strike with a thump into Radis's chair.

Radis stared at the board for a second, feeling dread well into his bowels. Then he leaned forward to hit the three keys that accessed the main computer several floors below in his offices, the hub of the Security Cadre of the Regnum. This machine was linked into the information storage and command structure of the entire Cadre. The only two other men in the galaxy that had such access watched the monitor flash as Radis's fingers flew over the keys, narrowing down through category and subcategory until the information sat there in bright, unequivocal letters before them. Since much of it was in the cryptic hieroglyphs of security lingo which Bolla would have trouble deciphering, Radis read it out.

"Sector Four—Pegasus system . . . Retor-quel—one of the new Seers. Autopsy says, 'cerebral aneurysm.' " Radis looked at Tyrees in time to see thin lips draw tighter over his teeth.

"Four days later—Pren-spel. Same system . . . He was an original, Vitar."

"I remember him," said Tyrees very softly.

"One hundred thirty-two standard years—old even for a Tercian. 'Viral infection—respiratory.' Very quick."

Radis had nothing more to say. He looked at Tyrees and knew. He *knew*. Tyrees's fist came crashing down on the chair arm and the monitor went blank.

"You should have realized, Radis. You should have told me."

"Yes." A weight mounted on the back of Radis's neck, pushing his head down. He blinked at the floor. "I didn't think. I just accepted it. There was too much going on—"

"Wait now, you two!" sputtered Bolla. "Just what *is* going on here?"

Tyrees rose slowly and walked to the balcony window. Bolla saw the blurred white face reappear against the black backdrop, saw the mouth open to voice one word.

"Murder," he said.

Three

The Seer's peril is twofold: he is as a lamb on the inward path to the heart of darkness, for he travels alone; he is as a lamb on the outward path also, for on it, he is blindly led.

—The Teraac

"THAT'S RIGHT. SURVEILLANCE teams with *every* Seer. I don't *care* how many there are. Priority One. Instruct the Vice Proctors immediately." Radis paused for the acknowledgment, staring down at the board as if it held chess pieces and his opponent's last move had just revealed an unexpected and devastating strategy. "A Special Directive to the VP, Sector Four: Dispatch Cadre Two's to investigate the deaths of the two Seers. Unlimited support. Emergency report procedures. Get on it now."

Radis closed the circuit. He looked up at Tyrees with blasted eyes. "Is there anything else we can do?"

"Yes." Tyrees was standing over him, but with a distracted air, like a man who knew he had forgotten something vital but didn't know what it was. Radis knew this was deceptive, for he had seen the look before in moments of crisis. He felt the charge in the air again—even Bolla felt it. Tyrees was alive again.

"Check on the whereabouts of every Seer—*every* Seer, Radis, during the time of those deaths."

Radis swallowed. He shook his head slowly. "I don't believe it, Vitar."

Tyrees's voice was calm. "You have to believe it. There's no alternative, unless . . ."

"An acolyte? A new adept? Is it possible?"

"I don't know. I think not, but check that out too. Canvass the Seers about their trainees. We're looking for someone . . . someone very special."

Radis sighed and nodded. "I'm sorry, Vitar. I should have been acting on this weeks ago."

"And so should I," said Tyrees. His head turned again, irresistibly, it seemed, to take in the night beyond the glass. "I never anticipated this, but it was probably inevitable. The Learning *humbles* most men, but *I* almost . . . I had myself for a warning. We will lose another Seer soon—we may have already."

Bolla had had enough. *"All right,"* he said. "All right, damn it!" He slapped a chubby knee. "What in the Maker's name have I been listening to here! I thought I was delivering an interesting problem in psychodynamics, and you two launch into some kind of—of *siege* reaction. What's going on? What's so unusual about two men dying of natural causes?"

"A Seer just doesn't die that way, Hans," said Tyrees.

"What do you mean? You two seem to be looking for an *assassin*—as if there were a knife sticking in the body!"

"There is, Doctor, only I didn't see it," muttered Radis. "Until you started talking about a New Covenant *without Seers*."

"Oh, I see. Very well. Thank you," said Bolla with polite sarcasm. "Now, will you spell it out for me? For an old, very feeble old man?"

Radis looked at him strangely. "You should have taken up the New Learning, Doctor."

Now Bolla was thoroughly exasperated. "What has that got to do—"

"A Seer is as aware of his bodily functions—*all* of them—as a conductor is of the instruments in his orchestra. A single false note is like a bomb going off, don't you see?''

Bolla was incredulous. ''You mean, he can't die of natural causes?''

''Of course he can—but not without warning, not without *knowing* it well in advance.''

''But—''

''A Seer's body holds no surprises for him, Hans,'' put in Tyrees. ''You should know that much by now.''

''Now wait one minute!'' Bolla slapped his knee again. ''Are you telling me, Pol, that you would know if you had a—a weak spot in an artery, one that might lead to an aneurysm?''

Tyrees nodded. ''Yes. For weeks, perhaps months. At my age I could probably repair it.''

Bolla stared at him, stared at the man he had known as a child, as if for the first time. Silver lines of perspiration formed in the deep creases on his forehead.

''I believe you,'' he whispered. ''It's true. It's true. I've seen enough . . . Why did you never speak of these things? Look at me!'' Fingers that were now trembling touched his sagging jowls, fell to his heavy man's breasts. ''Did you think I didn't need help?''

The hard, chiseled lines of Tyrees's ascetic face unlocked, softened. He looked to Radis, who could only shake his head. He walked slowly to a corner where a small crystal vase sat unadorned on its own slender table. Bolla's watery eyes followed him. He picked up the vase, carefully turning it in his fingers. It was simple, fragile, and quite beautiful, though far from rare and of no great value. He spoke from that distance.

''That would be too much, Hans. It takes years, sometimes a whole lifetime of dedicated training, for an average man to come to even the lowest levels. A very few have natural talents. The Tercian Seers were selected before puberty—and then they were blinded.'' He took his magnetic eyes from the vase and turned them to Bolla. ''Do you tell a little boy at a circus that tomorrow he will fly like the man on the trapeze?''

Bolla looked away and fumbled in the volumes of his robe until he pulled forth a square of white cloth which he used to mop his face. He made a noise into it that sounded like a chuckle, then blew his nose.

"Sorry, gentlemen. Very unbecoming of me. A weak moment there. I think I *knew* all of that, but I needed . . . needed to have it said." He smiled and turned in his chair to Radis, who was still bent, elbows on knees, with his eyes on the table board. "Radis, my boy. Tell me—how far have *you* come? Can you do those things? Can you fix up your innards like a space mechanic?"

Radis couldn't help laughing, but his laughter helped them all. He was able to look at Bolla fondly.

"No. I'm not a Seer, Doctor. But I can tinker with my breathing a bit. I can even put myself to sleep—especially if *you're* around." Then he sobered. "I wish I had more time. . . ."

"I too," said Tyrees from the corner of the room as he replaced the vase tenderly on its pedestal. Both of the others realized suddenly that they had never seen him pay attention to something so utterly without function. But it was Bolla who got them back on track, his no-nonsense intellect like a bloodhound returned to the scent.

"So you two think the two Seers were murdered. If their special abilities would preclude sudden, *natural* death, how could someone *make* it happen?"

"That's exactly the point," said Tyrees. "It had to have been induced—by someone whose 'abilities' were even greater than theirs."

For the second time that night Bolla was incredulous. "But that's impossible! You're saying that another *Seer* . . ."

"Yes—a *maverick*. Or someone, someone with the Learning but outside the New Covenant."

Bolla blew air violently out of bulging cheeks. "I wouldn't have thought either was possible."

"Nor I," said Tyrees shaking his head. "But your Anavex has taught us a lesson. We assumed that the New Covenant could be destroyed—but not perverted. Now we know better. Someone is trying to *use* it. Someone is trying to take over by destroying its leadership with the very skills it teaches.''

Bolla frowned in confusion. ''But I thought certain—certain moral precepts went along with that teaching. I remember thinking often to myself that Meta-sol—when any blood was shed—seemed to die a little himself.''

''You knew Meta-sol better than I thought,'' said Tyrees. ''But the New Covenant doesn't really 'teach' a moral code.'' He seemed about to say more, but with the gesture of a weary man, bent his neck, ran both palms slowly up his forehead and over his naked skull, and stopped speaking.

''Please, Vitar.'' Radis stood, an obscure look of pleading in his eyes. ''There's more to it than that.'' Tyrees dropped his hands, but only shrugged and turned away. Radis continued, choosing his words with difficulty. ''No moral code, no. But after a time, Doctor, after a time you . . . change. Your training puts you more and more on such, such *intimate* terms with yourself—*your own life*—that it's . . . well, it's frightening, in a way. Your life is so fragile, you see, so precarious.'' Unconsciously, Radis had cupped his hands and was staring into them.

''*All* life takes on sanctity then. It's a miracle, and yet so vulnerable!'' He noticed his hands then, and laced his fingers with some embarrassment. ''That's morality, isn't it?''

''That's *mortality*.''

''What?'' Radis was startled by Tyrees's remark. He was again standing in the corner near the delicate vase, glaring at them. His eyes were blue flames.

''And you come to the point where your mind finally *joins* your body—to fight consciously what the flesh has always been fighting on the brute level of the cell. Mortality. And you can't win that fight.''

Radis wanted desperately to refute these words, but he could not. They came from his Vitar, and they came with the understated passion of certainty. Besides, those eyes would brook no rebuke; they rooted him in silence—until they fell to the vase.

Almost instantly Radis felt the air shiver, felt it the way a sleeping cat feels his whiskers touched. In a second or two there was a crinkling spit of sound as the crystal vase shattered. Tyrees stood darkly over the small pile of fragments, one of which still rocked daintily on its own curve.

It took Bolla a moment to realize what had happened; when he did, he scowled at Tyrees.

"I'm still worried about you, Pol. You're not usually given to useless dramatics—especially destructive ones."

Tyrees picked up the rocking fragment, sighed, and dropped it back into the pile. "No—you're right. I apologize. And Radis is right too." He moved back to join them as if nothing had happened. "It's difficult to believe that a Seer could become an executioner. But we must accept the possibility simply because there are few others."

Radis nodded. "It's almost as hard to believe that a Seer could train an acolyte with a killer's mind and not know it."

"We *all* have killer's minds, Radis."

With that, Tyrees walked away from them, his voice trailing behind. "Call me when you have something."

He stepped into the mouth of the dim hall that led to Shaamlik's chamber.

Four

Laugh at your own despair. It is a silly thing. True despair is reserved for immortals. Laughter is our defiance of them, our nobility.

—*The Sayings of Meta-sol*

THE CITADEL WAS a structure of Brobdingnagian proportions, by design dominating the vast city of lesser buildings that housed the intricate bureaucracy of a galactic government. The offices of the Cadre Proctor—Central Headquarters—were also in the Citadel, but so cut off and distinct from the other levels above (one reserved for the Council and the topmost for the Vitar) that they might have been on another world. Here, all was bustle and hum, with dedicated staff working always within the vibrations of a highly pitched strum of decision. Here was gathered the net, the tenuous but powerful filaments of law that held the Regnum together. Central HQ was the gatherer, the guardian of that net. It commanded the loyalty of excruciatingly trained and talented personnel who were speckled lightly across several hundred light-years of space—in practical terms the most cohesive cadre of men and women that history had ever seen fit to allow. But the Cadre depended less upon that prodigious loyalty for its strength than upon its privilege and capacity to gather like humble fishermen an infinitely various, slippery haul—information. This was stored, monitored, and analyzed. Most law breakers were spotted in this fashion.

The Regnum was divided into eleven sectors, each with its Vice Proctor commanding a Sector HQ through which the Cadre pulled its data from the star systems. The Cadre had at least one FSO, a Field Support Office, in every star system.

In matters of Regnum law, which regulated interplanetary affairs, the Council and the Cadre were supreme; local autonomy prevailed otherwise.

So it was that through several hundred disparate worlds, for over a thousand years, a semblance of order was maintained. But that order had always been a thin and brittle layer of ice on the river of time—one constantly fissured by greed. The New Covenant was the first promise of purpose unalloyed by base immediacies, but the Security Cadre still had its historical purpose—to keep the law.

So it was that the latest Cadre Proctor, very young for the title though he had risen to the highest field rank of Cadre One before the coup, was an anomaly. He was Cadre—and he was an acolyte of the New Covenant. Each had noble purpose; each by its nature demanded total commitment. This thought never left Radis, never ceased to torture him. When he stole time to meditate with Pan-sol, the one Seer in the system, he itched; when—by far more time consuming—he functioned as Cadre Proctor, he itched. In both he felt a need to serve his Vitar, but he knew Tyrees wanted him where he was—pulling in the net.

He had just finished going over the dozens of reports connected with the Seer investigation and was headed out of his office to keep his appointment with Tyrees when he came upon one of his administrative assistants in conversation with a caped officer.

"I'm sorry, sir," she was saying, "but the Cadre Proctor won't be seeing anyone for—oh."

"That's right," said Radis, barely glancing in their direction as he made for an exit. "Make an appointment."

"Excuse me—sir."

The voice stopped him. He turned to see a tall, slender man with crisp brown hair and the solid black collar cording of a Cadre One. Silent alarms sounded in his head even before he felt the telltale tingle in the air. The gray eyes had delayed recognition—so had the hair and the dark eyebrows.

"I really must see you, sir. It's quite urgent."

"Uh, yes—well, come in then." He turned to lead the man back to his office. His admin assistant was annoyed.

"Sir, you haven't forgotten . . ."

"No. I'll take care of it."

When his office door hissed closed behind them, Radis was unable to contain his bewilderment. He stared at the now smiling Number One from head to toe and shook his head.

"All right, I give up. Why?"

"I fooled them, didn't I?

"My people?" said Radis, jerking his head toward the door. "Most of them have never seen you in the flesh, but I guess you pass. But remember, I'm the only person around here who's supposed to look a Number One in the eye." He stabbed a button on his desk that said to his minions outside, "I have just ceased to exist," and asked his question again. *"Why, Vitar?"*

Tyrees fingered the soft, dark fabric of his cape. "You know, this is hard to admit—but I've missed the feel of this uniform."

"That's your answer?"

"No, Radis. We'll get to that later. First I want to hear what you have. I suspect it's nothing much."

Radis's eyebrows went up. "You're right, unfortunately."

"I'm right because 'fortune' has so little to do with it." Tyrees flexed his shoulders, as if getting the feel of the cape again. "This is going to be bad, Radis. I can smell it."

"Well, we may still be operating on a false assumption."

"It's the only *possible* assumption—until we can come up with another explanation for those Seers' deaths. I don't think we will." Tyrees fiddled with the contact lenses. "I'm not used to these things yet."

When Tyrees raised his head again, Radis felt the familiar shock. The blue heat of those eyes dominated—even more than he had realized—everything they touched. He began his report.

"We've turned up nothing in connection with the two Seers, Vitar. No 'visitors' in common that we've been able to unearth, though the time gap doesn't help. I've ordered more comprehensive autopsies—but that won't help either, will it? Not if we're right."

"Get to the crucial stuff, Radis."

Radis sighed. "I know what you're thinking. The killer needed at least six weeks for a round trip, unless he was already in the system, and no other Seer was. We checked every one, Vitar—over a hundred—and not one was absent for that period of time. We are certain of that. So there's no maverick, no rogue Seer. That only leaves your theory about a gifted trainee, and reports so far are all negative, but we're still working on it."

As Radis spoke, Tyrees had been wandering about the large office, poking and prodding absently. In spite of the crisis, Radis felt good about his presence and the uniform. He had rejoined the brotherhood. His demeanor showed signs of the old, at times infamous, Tyrees tenacity.

"I hope you're right about the six weeks, Radis, but you are going to have to narrow it to a few days."

Radis was stunned. *"Days?* Surely that's—"

"Impossible? You believe that, after three years on Condor?"

"Oh shit." Radis felt his face drain. He leaned back to the edge of his desk and slumped against it. "The pathways. You think he might be able to use the intergalactic pathways."

"It can't be ruled out," said Tyrees quietly.

Space vessels traveled the galactic pathways routinely, creating the faster-than-light effect that allowed the Regnum to exist. Intergalactic pathways, however, could not be detected by even the most sophisticated navigation equipment. This simple fact led to the takeover of a stellar empire by a single ship under the command of a rebel Cadre One. He could "read" the intergalactic pathways when even Meta-sol could not; he could place the ship—without danger of atomizing it—on the invisible roads that rainbowed through the Milky Way from out of the depths of the Greater Void. His were smooth highways, theirs rutted and rocky goat trails; he had wings, they had feet. He was an outlaw, but he and Condor mocked them from above. He swooped down when and where he wished for the Birthings— the seeding of the Seers throughout the galaxy, and the spawning of the New Covenant.

Radis was shaken, because to him, this was unthinkable. *A power that matched the Vitar's.* This he had not imagined, but the possibility did not seem to bother Tyrees.

"Vitar, is that why you're wearing the uniform?"

"That's part of it. I have to go out in the field, Radis. There are some things your men—even you—are not equipped to see. Not dealing with a Seer."

"That is bad security." Radis could see one thing: that Tyrees was only too happy to render this particular judgment.

"I move as a Cadre One. That will be security enough."

"Move *where?*"

"Nowhere at the moment, Radis." Tyrees smiled. "This was just a dry run. If your people didn't recognize me, no one would."

"Except our killer."

Tyrees smiled more broadly and executed a deep bow. Radis didn't like this uncharacteristic display. He had seen his Vitar, as he would a diamond, through many facets lately, more than he knew existed. It unnerved him. The feeling was exacerbated further by the knowledge that Tyrees could no doubt read his current emotional profile as another would read a chart, should he wish to do so. Putting a hard clamp on his feelings, he moved behind his desk and sat.

"You have a plan of action? We're waiting for something?"

Tyrees looked at him darkly. "Yes. The next Seer's death. Then you close the planet down. No off-world travel. Then we go there—fast."

Radis nodded. It was typical of Tyrees: hard-nosed, direct, logical—and daring; daring an incursion of the unpredictable more than anything else.

"And if such a thing is not forthcoming? The Seers do have the best protection we can give them."

"Then I go to the source—Tercet."

"Tercet! In the Maker's name, why?"

"Because that is all there is left." Tyrees reached into the underside of his cape and withdrew a small, very antiquated book. It was pliable, bound in what could only be the treated hide of some animal. He handled it tenderly, holding it up. "This is Meta-sol's diary. I've read it often since his death. Two days ago I remembered a line—a single line. Meta-sol was writing about the last Gathering. Those were the last of my days on Tercet. The Seers were called together, as they were ritually every three years or in a time of crisis. My training under Meta-sol was over. He summoned them to see me, to witness my investiture. I was to be the first non-Tercian Seer, and the youngest by fifty years."

Tyrees paused, his eyes losing focus. Radis took mental note of yet another new facet in the diamond—nostalgia. Could it be that this very special man—now in his late forties—was finally a victim of the more fallible human indulgences that he had hitherto denied himself?

"And the line, Vitar?" prompted Radis.

"Yes. It might have no bearing, Radis, but it can't be ignored. It's in Tercian, of course—I'll translate." Tyrees opened the old book at a marker. "I'll start earlier to give you the context. It goes—'I am proud of my new son. His powers thrill and frighten me, but we will learn more at the Gathering.'" Tyrees's hand rose to touch his forehead, covering his face. "Here is the line: 'I am ashamed that Uni-shad refuses to come, will not lend his great sight, for this Gathering could mark new beginnings.'" He looked up. "That's it."

Radis felt his own pulse quicken. "This man, this Uni-shad, he must be a Seer?"

"Or he would not be expected at the Gathering."

"And he was not with the others on Condor."

"No. I had always assumed that Meta-sol had brought *all* the Seers. Remember: we had every reason to believe that Tercet was about to be reduced to a cinder—*would have been*—had we not been warned by Bolla in enough time to escape with what the Chairman intended to destroy—me and the Seers."

"And Meta-sol never mentioned him?"

Tyrees shook his head.

"But . . . it just doesn't sound like Meta-sol. Why would he leave a Seer behind if he might be obliterated?"

"That is the question that troubles me. I'm going to find out."

"But the other Seers—*some* of them—must know this man! I'll get Pan-sol to—"

Tyrees held up a hand. "I've asked him. He remembers the man vaguely by name. He assumed that since he didn't come with us, he had died. Keep in mind that Pan-sol is young, a Seer for only a year or so before we left Tercet."

"Then we must question the others, Vitar!"

"Of course. But since there *are* no others in our system, I think it wise to wait until—"

A sharp buzzer sounded. Radis was irritated as he reached for a key on his desk, but he kept it out of his voice, knowing that the signal had to be important.

"Yes?"

"Message burst, sir. Sector Eight. Priority One."

"Seer team?"

"Yes sir. Singletary."

"Pipe it in." He looked up at Tyrees. "I hope this isn't what you've been waiting for, Vitar."

Tyrees said nothing. The monitor on Radis's desk began to break into fuzzy light. Radis swiveled it so both could watch. Lines of words appeared and began to roll upward. The format was one with which both observers were intimately familiar.

* * *

Field Agent's Report—Ttig Hal, Cadre Two, Surveillance

Sector Eight

Assignment Directive
• Surveil and protect Las-trom, Seer, Singletary

Report Procedure
• Routine—weekly
• Emergency—immediate, Priority One, CP direct

Emergency Report

Seer Las-trom suddenly fallen ill. Medic's diagnosis inconclusive but subject critical. Vital signs low and dropping. Request instruction.

TH—C2

Tyrees smoothed the cape on his lap. "Now it's certain. We are under attack, Radis. Get *Condor* ready. And shut down that planet."

"Need we be so drastic?" said Radis with some hesitation. "It's only one man."

"I'd like to think that the Chairman once said something like that about *me*." There was no trace of humor in Tyrees's voice.

"I take your point, Vitar—but the Seer is *sick,* not dead."

"You don't take my point. The threat is greater than we thought. The report said nothing about an attempt on the Seer's life. Our killer was operating at a *distance*, Radis. Hal was totally unaware of it. Do you know what that means?"

The thought was spawning in Radis's mind before Tyrees finished speaking. The unthinkable was again pushing insidiously through the suddenly tender wall of his mind. As it pushed, it took on the rank smell of his own fear.

"From a distance? You think he can kill a man—a *Seer*— from a distance?"

"Yes." Tyrees stood and looked down at Radis calmly, but his eyes were coated with ice.

"I'm coming with you." Radis stood also. His expression was defiantly pleading.

"No. You are too crucial here, and I need your backup."

"You need my backup in the field," said Radis. There was a thin blade of desperation in his voice which Tyrees must have caught, for he did something uncharacteristic—yet another facet. He reached and touched Radis's cheek for a moment with his fingertips.

"Your man on Singletary—the Number Two, Ttig Hal—I trained with him. There's no one better, and I trust him as much as I trust you." With that, he turned and headed for the door.

"Vitar!"

Tyrees turned and smiled. "How many times have I asked you not to call me that?"

Radis sighed heavily. "Take Bolla, then. I can watchdog the Council for him."

"All right. Tell him, will you? And look in on Shaamlik while we're gone?"

Radis nodded, and the black cape swirled out the door. He moved woodenly to his desk chair, trying to frame mentally the instructions for Singletary and the preparation of *Condor*. First, he had to cut viciously at the thing pushing through the wall of his mind.

Five

Taken each as one, man's life is a closed circle. One man is driven, or seeks inward; another is driven, or seeks outward. The curved line of the circle strangles the nether man, for he is easy prey to the pressure from without; the same sharp line severs the man of action from self-knowledge. Thousands of generations have made it so. We must open the circle—or perish.

—The Teraac

CONDOR.

She was every man's fondest wish. Imagination is flight—she was flight beyond the reachless boundaries of the universe. Freedom is speed—she was speed that denied the senses and the calculations of reason. Power is invincibility—she could not be bested except by a number of her own kind; there were few of them, and they were her sisters.

Space vessels like *Condor* were hideously expensive, and an entire generation in the making. In the distant past her forerunners were the great battleships or aircraft carriers that plied oceans instead of space; unlike her, they were subject to the ironic paradox of conflict: they were too powerful, too valuable to risk losing, so they were seldom placed well enough to dictate the flux of crucial events. *Condor* had been an exception because she had been the *only* weapon of the rebels, and because her masters were daring.

She was still manned by the crew that brought Tyrees home to his destiny. That was two short years ago, and her name was already the stuff of legend. When Tyrees and Bolla returned aboard without fanfare or sentiment, the chests of the crew still expanded—less from a memory of great accomplishment than that of an awesome fear, shared and overcome. They knew that there was no stronger bond. They loved Tyrees, not because they thought him a god, but because he had given them under common cause the rarest of gifts: the opportunity to taste as it welled from their viscera, the acid tide of death—and the strength to force it back.

They were three years on the run, outlaws whose only home was *Condor* and the black Void, and the experience had made them into an odd group: an efficient, tightly knit team when aboard *Condor*, but with a grim cast and unsettled air when their feet walked on finite soil. Each and every one was treated as a hero now, but they surprised themselves by discovering quickly that it didn't compensate for the drug mix of fear and meaning in space. Somehow, they had lost the great gift of ease.

Condor was virtually hanging in space outside of the plane of the galaxy, but only a few parsecs from Regnum. She had come there in only a few hours under conventional power. Tyrees had taken the command chair from the captain, and the bridge waited with contained anticipation. They were like religious initiates awaiting the comfort and confirmation of a secret, holy rite.

"Ready, NAVCOM?"

"Yes, sir." The woman at the navigation console looked over one shoulder at him, her hands caressing the keys with the light and knowing touch of a mother. Bolla stood to one side and slightly behind Tyrees, morosely glum. One hand held onto the back of the command chair. Even three-quarter G seemed too much for him, but he watched Tyrees carefully.

Tyrees raised his eyes to the large screen that dominated the bridge. It tilted down toward them from above and contained mostly blackness because it projected a preselected segment of space outside of the galactic plane. It was a framed image of the Void. Only a few, cold specks, tiny pinpricks of light, hinted that the nullity was incomplete. Silence entered the bridge and stretched. The dull background hum of the instrumentation only deepened it. Bolla fidgeted. It had stretched into a painful thinness when he saw Tyrees's eyes flicker, waver. Their blue was faded, washed with white.

Alarmed, Bollar stepped in front of the command chair, blocking the screen. Tyrees blinked and half lifted a hand. Bolla spoke in a low voice.

"Pol . . . Pol, are you all right?"

The hand fell, but Bolla noted the shallow breathing.

"Pol?"

Several seconds passed before Tyrees responded. "Yes . . . yes, I'm fine, Hans." His breathing deepened, evened out. "Some difficulty . . . difficulty concentrating."

Bolla frowned. "Is it harder now?"

"No. It's . . . No. It's all right, Doctor. I'll start again. Please." Bolla was inclined to protest, but he caught the stares of some of the bridge crew, waved vaguely at nothing in particular, and moved back to one side of the command chair.

Tyrees began again, this time closing his eyes and going deep into his relaxed mode. Bolla watched the muscles on the back of his neck sink into the flesh. The eyes reopened, and as Bolla had seen many times before when they gazed at the overhead screen, they glazed over, gaining opacity as if layers of glass were being fitted, one at a time. The voice came in a few moments—a slow, sedated monotone, slightly slurred.

"J quadrant . . . y matrix . . . point, point zero . . . four, two . . . nine. X matrix . . . nine point . . . zero, zero . . . five, one."

He stopped and breathed heavily, with some effort it seemed to Bolla, as he waited for the confirmation from NAVCOM. A tiny beep sounded when her fingers stopped tapping the keys. The coordinates of the invisible pathway had been fed into the navigation computer.

"Ready, sir."

"Adjust."

A quiet staccato of cryptic instructions and confirmations, a deceptively casual bouncing ball of human voices swept the bridge as *Condor* was maneuvered precisely into position. This part of the process was the same even for galactic pathways. If either the original coordinates or the delicate positioning were slightly off when the gravity field was dropped, two results were possible: the ship would "slide off" the pathway and wallow like a rowboat in a high sea for a time; or it would take the path "sideways" and never reappear in conventional space. No one, of course, ever knew what actually happened to the ship in the latter case, though this was rare for a trained crew and the minutely charted galactic pathways.

By the time the patter ended, Tyrees was breathing more easily, though Bolla took note of the sheen of oily sweat on the skin of his skull.

"Ready, sir," said NAVCOM.

"Drop the gravity field."

"Dropping field, sir."

No space crew ever wasted time worrying at this point, because once gravity was erased for the ride on the pathway, a serious failure would never be registered. *Condor* shuddered, and it was over. The screen flashed erratically before finding new resolution. There were no stars embedded in black slate—unless the multicolored streaks were indeed stars. No one knew. The screen was now a child's smear of watery paints that told nothing except for the indication of movement in a constant direction as washes of color swept over and over the lines of the smear.

They were on an intergalactic pathway—different from those inside the galaxy in ways that the best scientists had not yet fathomed—catapulted at a rate measured in light-years per hour into the Greater Void. Somewhere in the abyss, at a point only Tyrees could identify, he would take them off the path simply by raising the gravity field. He would then place them on another intersecting pathway for the plunge back into their spangle in space called the Milky Way. What would take *Condor* to journey to Singletary on this super highway a few days, would take those on the back roads of the galactic pathways weeks.

As he always did, Bolla was logging mentally the observable state of Pol Tyrees as the bridge settled down to routine function. He did not like what he saw: the hands moving slowly along the arms of the command chair to pull the body forward; the body leaning into the effort to rise; the eyes still not cleared of their layers of glass; the voice ordinary, without its usual magnetic timbre.

"Take the chair, Captain."

The captain left his station at the FIRECOM console and came forward. Bolla resisted the impulse to help as Tyrees stepped slowly to the deck from the raised dais. He followed as Tyrees walked with the careful precision of a drunkard off the bridge.

By the time they arrived at his quarters—only the captain's, by tradition, were closer to the bridge—a mere minute later, and Tyrees had settled into his old spot before a master terminal, he had fully recovered. He looked at Bolla with a wan smile.

"Just like old times, eh, Doctor?"

Bolla lifted his jaw high to rub at its opened creases. He grunted softly, like a mastiff relaxing after a false alarm, and fingered the wig of brown hair that lay at the foot of the bunk.

"No, Pol. It's not like old times," he said. "It *is* getting harder, isn't it?"

Tyrees hesitated, obviously reluctant to respond. He shook his head, rose from his chair, and moved to the bunk. "Not in the way you think. It's not the actual . . . effort. I seem to have more difficulty concentrating. It *has* been two years since we spread *Condor's* wings last, Hans."

"Bullshit," said Bolla softly. "I know how you can read bodies, Pol. You could catch men in a lie even before the Learning—you were famous for it as an interrogator in the Cadre. But you didn't see *yourself* in the command chair a few minutes ago. When *I* can read *you*, my young friend, it means something serious."

Tyrees looked blankly at him for a moment, the blue eyes

almost as painfully burning as usual now. Then he closed them and leaned back on the bunk.

"That obvious, was it?"

"To me it was," said Bolla. "I have my own modest expertise, you know."

Tyrees's wrist bent limply over the edge of the bunk. Bolla reached and grasped it delicately, fingers probing. The eyes opened as it was snatched away.

"All right," sighed Bolla, "*you* tell me."

"Tell you what?"

"Your pulse rate—what is it? I know you can tell me."

Tyrees shrugged. "About normal. Low seventies."

Bolla smiled evilly, the smile he used to use when he caught a postgraduate plagiarizing. "Oh, my goodness!" he said with mock coyness. "Imagine! Little ol' me catching the *Vitar* in a lie!" Then he laughed, an almost silent exercise which was often caricatured, for his ample cheeks bellowed and collapsed in quick rhythms as short snorts burst from his nostrils. By the time he recovered, Tyrees was smiling ruefully himself.

"What's *your* normal rate, Pol? Forty-five . . . fifty?"

"About," said Tyrees, with some irritation. "Okay, you're right. I was struggling out there. I told you. It's a matter of concentration—nothing I can't handle."

"Pol." Bolla's tone was deadly serious, but flecked with pleading. "I am a psychologist. And I know you—as well as anyone does. You were afraid."

Tyrees said nothing. He swung his feet off the bunk and took the two strides to his master console, pulling a chair under him.

"Talk to me, Pol."

"Go away, Doctor. I've got to study the reports on Singletary."

Bolla ignored him. "Listen to me, Pol." He moved to stand behind Tyrees. He noted that the powerful, slender hands lay inert near the board, and took hope. He wanted to lift his own and put them on Tyrees's shoulders, but he resisted the impulse.

"You're fond of telling Radis that you're not a god—yet you try to behave like one. You are a unique man, but still a *man. Men become afraid,* Pol."

The small room swallowed up his words. The silence swallowed up his words. With sudden poignance, Bolla was hit by a sense of where they were: encapsulated by a few molecules of plasteel; plunging outward into the depthless black of the Greater Void; absurdly distant from a flicker of a galaxy they called home; artificially, delicately sustained on a plane of time and space that no one understood. He, too, became afraid. He looked at the back of the pale skull below him, and his heart flooded. He raised his hands and put them on Tyrees's shoulders.

Slowly, as if the motion had been carefully considered, Tyrees nodded.

"Yes, Hans. I am afraid." His voice was a bare whisper. "But I don't think you can understand."

"Tell me."

The skull moved only slightly around toward him. "What words do I use?"

Bolla had to summon all the calm of his years. "The ones that come closest." Silence. He increased the pressure of his hands on the shoulders. "The time track. It started with the time track, didn't it?"

Another slow, deliberate nod. Another whisper. "Yes."

"There was a cost. A *high* cost."

"Yes."

"Tell me."

"I was an addict, Hans. I was destroying myself."

Bolla shivered. "Tell me."

The whisper, like the first trickle of water that had oozed through the thick wall of a dam, gained urgency, took on volume and momentum.

"I was a *rider,* Hans. I rode on a current like . . . like a savage in a frail canoe. I couldn't control it, unless I kept near the shore—a second into the future. . . . No, less than that. Much less than that. Chronometers can't measure how small ahead was the time I could move safely into. I was still . . . *there*. Everything was the same except it *stopped*. People turned to statues!''

Bolla felt the drug of relief wash over his anxiety. He slid his hands from Tyrees's shoulders and kept his voice calm, deliberate.

''That's what happened during the coup. You and Meta-sol, you were able to get on the time track when the Chairman was presenting us like caged circus freaks to the public.'' He grimaced at the memory of the indignity. ''You could do anything you like, then? Wouldn't the time eventually, ah, catch up?''

Tyrees nodded. ''That seems logical. But I've been 'close to shore' like that for over an hour and couldn't see any difference. The statues never moved; my timer never turned over a single second.''

''You can't sustain that state.''

''No. Not indefinitely,'' said Tyrees. ''Fatigue sets in. Concentration goes. You lose it. Meta-sol could only hang on for a few minutes.''

Now the conversation was taking Bolla, rather than the man. He was struck for the thousandth time by a thought that his crushing responsibilities over the last two years—or his fears— had always pushed aside. He pulled his shirt away from the dampness under his armpits and voiced it.

''Pol . . . you can alter the future.''

Tyrees swung his chair around. His face looked older. ''No, Hans, I can't *change* it. I can *create* it.''

Bolla moved heavily to the bunk and sat. He rubbed his temples with the palms of his hands. ''Oh dear, oh dear,'' he muttered. ''It's a wonder you're not a blazing, blubbering lunatic, Pol.''

Tyrees smiled sadly and shook his head. He seemed to have recovered completely, except for a quality of lassitude that attenuated the slashes of silence between his words.

"It's not that bad. Besides, I would have to be at exactly the place, and exactly the time, and I can affect only what—literally—happens *next*. The very next instant."

"I know. I saw it happen," said Bolla.

In his memory he saw again the bizarre collage of images that the mind could only attempt to deny—the same images that were sent through the galaxy via the live cameras. Tyrees and Meta-sol disappeared like apparitions of the air, and the whole scene before his eyes kept shifting from one insane grotesquerie to another: the guards, disarmed, sitting back to back in a children's circle on the floor of the stage; the Chairman discovering his own hairy-ugly nakedness exposed to the audience; Tyrees and Meta-sol appearing and reappearing among the changing sets like farcical stage hands in a doctored holofilm production; the Chairman again, gibbering like a monkey, still naked, as he perched high on a ceiling beam.

Yes, it was a miracle, thought Bolla. What did these things mean to the man who sat opposite him now? Perhaps he was indeed a god? Bolla shook his head like a dog with a new collar.

"The coup. Was that the last time you used the time track?"

Tyrees's chin jerked up slightly. He, too, had been lost in thought. "Yes. And you needn't worry on that account." Bolla felt the blue eyes pierce. "I will never escape the present again."

Bolla was confused. "But why? Are you afraid of—"

Tyrees laughed without humor. "It's not what you're thinking, Hans. I'm not afraid for my sanity."

"Then what? You said—you said you were *destroying* yourself."

Tyrees swiveled his chair back to the console. The silence stretched out until Bolla thought there would be no answer. He could feel the presence of the Void again. As he was on the verge of another prompt, Tyrees's voice came back to him—slowly, with poisonous calm.

"You saw what it did to me. Before the coup. Not the track

close to shore. Radis saw it even more clearly, because he helped to pull me out.''

Bolla drew a deep breath. "When we were prisoners in that mansion? I hardly saw you at all, for weeks at a time. You kept to your room. But anybody could see the . . . changes in you. That was when you—left the shore?''

Bolla watched the back of the pale skull nod. "There doesn't seem to be any in between. I rode out, Hans. Far out. I watched stars fade and die. I watched galaxies form out of gas and dust. I didn't want to come back and just . . . live.'' A soft exhalation, an almost silent sigh of resignation dropped the back of his head down. "You can't understand it.''

"Try, Pol. Try to tell me.'' The wetness at Bolla's armpits was now copied at his groin and in the small of his back. The quiet, controlled voice resumed; a judge's voice.

"All that I saw was so beautiful—and horrible. All that I saw . . . all that I saw—*diminished* me. It made me insignificant. It made *humanity* insignificant. I wallowed in it. I saw everything being born and eaten up. But *I* wasn't being eaten up, you see—not while I was on the time track—so I never wanted to come back. *Off* it, that is *exactly* what was happening to me. Being eaten up. Radis found me one night—I don't know how long it had been since I had slept or taken food. There wasn't much left of me. It was mostly his shock that brought me around, I guess. He thought all of it was my reaction to our capture then, and the failure of the New Covenant—and Shaamlik. In a way, all that was true too.''

Bolla's spine was shooting him obscure signals. He shifted on the bunk, scraping at his mind for composure. Something in Tyrees's words brushed nerve ends in dark places, nerve ends that were rarely touched.

"I suppose you are saying that nothing—even a whole galaxy full of sentient life—has much meaning.''

"Very well. That'll do, I suppose.''

Bolla struggled for his professorial manner. "You are aware, of course, that such a thought is almost as ancient as thought itself. Many philosophers—''

"No philosopher ever saw what I saw," said Tyrees sardonically.

Bolla was stopped briefly. After a time he said, "Nevertheless, I think you have seen—much more powerfully—what all men suspect is there."

"Perhaps."

Bolla felt utterly lost. He grabbed at a straw. "Tell me," he said, "one more thing. What do you think Meta-sol would say to you right now?"

Tyrees's shoulders twitched in irritation. "Hans—"

"Please. Indulge me. Think about it carefully."

Long moments passed before Tyrees swiveled the chair to face Bolla again. Expressionless, he reached into a cranny of the bulkhead and retrieved an ancient, gnarled stick of wood polished to that unique, dull smoothness that only years of the touching of human hands can produce. Bolla recognized Meta-sol's cane.

Tyrees stood it on the floor between his knees, both hands atop its knobbed end. He bent his back to lean over it in a pose that struck a single, deep chord of grief in Bolla's chest. The voice that came from Tyrees's lips was Meta-sol's voice—low but resonant, as always veined with a trace of humor, as always with a trace of sadness.

"Ahh, yes. You have yet much to learn, Pol of the hidden stars." Tyrees's head moved from side to side in a perfect imitation of the old Tercian's gesture of mock surprise. "Stay with us a while yet. Temper your power with wisdom. You will one day learn that a man is born only to discover what he is meant to be. Do that. You are stronger than the darkness."

Tyrees settled back and fingered the cane, now smiling his own smile. For once Bolla was not bemused by the vague metaphor of Tercian speech. It touched him benignly, in a way similar, but antithetical, to the deadly brushing of his nerve ends.

Six

The Learning is richest when the darkest depths are plumbed, but it is there, too, that the horror lies. Upon this paradox rests our destiny.

—The Teraac

CONDOR'S PLUNGE BACK out of the Greater Void was a scream of silence, for that immensity of perfect denial would permit not even sound.

She slid off the pathway with barely a shudder and opened her wings, flexing them for the feel of her power. She was back in her element now, banking with grace and confidence as she targeted on Singletary. The captain was in the command chair flanked by Bolla and Tyrees, who had once again been transformed into a Cadre One. It made the members of the bridge crew uneasy—after their years as outlaws, they had come to associate that uniform with an implacable enemy. The captain was instructing TELCOM.

"Identify us as Cadre Transport under Council Order. We are here pursuing an investigation which requires data gathered by the Cadre FSO."

Tyrees's preference was to make landfall with as little fuss as possible, but *Condor* herself was far too conspicuous—one of the Regnum's irreplaceable class XL's—to carry that too far;

hence the Council Order. Singletary had been one of the bastions of the old regime. She and the Chairman had profited greatly from their mutual wallowing at the galactic trough while other planets were being muscled slowly back to hoe-and-shovel economies. As with so many other worlds, the New Covenant had nevertheless taken hold here among the populace, so Singletary's wealthy ruling class had thus far fought their newly forced adherence to the letter of Regnum law only with hollow cries of outrage.

When the protocol of communications leading to *Condor's* orbit of Singletary was completed, the captain ordered the shuttle readied and turned to Tyrees.

"You can head down in a few minutes, sir."

"Thank you, Captain. We'll be in touch through the FSO— Ttig Hal, Cadre Two."

"Yes sir . . . uh, what about emergencies? I gather that Singletary is not our most friendly supporter."

"I don't expect any problems, Captain, but if we should go more than twelve hours without contact, pull out of orbit and message the Cadre Proctor."

"A two-way burst will take several hours, sir."

Tyrees had been about to leave, but the look of concern on the captain's face stopped him. Bolla nodded.

"He's right, Pol. The temptation may be too much if they should discover that they have the Vitar in their hands."

Tyrees smiled. "Very well. Message *them* after twelve hours. Tell them if they don't produce Dr. Bolla and me, you'll melt the whole planet down for scrap. Say those were my orders."

The captain's mouth fell open. "Do—Do I follow through on that?"

"Of course not. Contact the CP."

The shuttle journey and landing were routine, except that Bolla, absorbed as always in his careful observation of Tyrees, read strain in the lines near the eyes. In spite of what he had been told, Bolla had been inclined to reserve judgment on the maverick Seer theory; watching Tyrees now, he began to change his mind. This was the old Tyrees: those unfathomable powers of mind and body keyed high, expecting nothing, alert for anything.

When the shuttle ramp door fell away, an imposing figure was revealed standing on the spaceport apron. He was of average height, but the breadth of chest and shoulders and neck, the thickness of leg and forearm, made him appear squat. Everything about him was blockish, including his face and, as Tyrees well and fondly knew, his personality. Ttig Hal, Cadre Two, was looking up at them with a strange expression on his face. The wide, powerful stance, the bull's jaw and puggish nose, suggested a strength of will that was habitual, but at this moment, the eyes watching Tyrees descend the ramp were watery, the lips unsteady.

Bolla could only see Tyrees's back as he came to the bottom of the ramp and stood silently a few feet from Hal. In the background were two other caped figures bearing the green collar piping of Operations officers—Cadre Fours. Bolla felt excluded, irrelevant, a tourist gazing at a famous painting from a strange world. The small plaque beneath would read simply, "Four Figures Caped in Black." Singletary's diffuse sunlight and fuzzed, mottled sky seemed to place the four men on an inaccessible plane where decisions of impossible moment were about to be made.

A soft breeze touched Bolla's cheek—cool, oxygen rich— and he blinked. The spell was broken. Hal's forearm came across his body above the waist, forming a rigid line ending in a fist.

"Ttig Hal, Cadre Two. Welcome to Singletary . . . sir."

Tyrees returned the salute. "Hello, Ttig. It's been a long, long time." From Hal, a slow nod. "You're not supposed to recognize me, Ttig."

Hal looked at the ground and smiled like a shy boy. "No, sir."

Minutes later two Cadre ground cars sped through

Singletary's capital using the clear emergency lanes. The two Operations officers were in the lead car. Hal "drove" the second, though it was on full automatic.

"We'll just be a few minutes, sir," he said, without looking to the backseat.

Tyrees said in a flat voice, "You haven't called me anything but Pol since we were fifteen, Ttig."

Hal turned. His eyes shone with delight. "As you said, that was a long, long time ago—Pol." When he smiled, his face became archetypal—the big-toothed bonhomme, comic and friend of all. Bolla had the feeling that the smile was not allowed to break often. "Are you really a god?"

Tyrees laughed. It was a rare sound, for it was unmitigated humor. Bolla was glad to hear it. He knew that in his younger years Tyrees had known only two friends, and this man was one of them. The other was Dace Sestus—and Tyrees had killed him.

"Tell me something, Ttig. About six years ago—just before I was sent to Tercet—the grapevine had it that you made Cadre One. What happened?"

The toothy smile disappeared. "You don't know?" Tyrees frowned and shook his head. "Come to think of it, why should you? I was the mission control officer on the ship that was sent to obliterate Tercet, Pol."

Tyrees winced. He thought of his bluff about Singletary.

"You disobeyed the order?"

"Not exactly. The captain wanted to shoot and run. I forced him to land and investigate first—against the letter of the mission order. When it was established that you and the Seers were gone, even the Chairman had to rescind. I was busted to a Two before I got back to Sector HQ."

Tyrees expelled a slow breath. He parted his cape, putting both hands on his knees. "Thanks, Ttig."

"Unnecessary," said Hal, turning to face forward again. "I would have done the same thing even if you weren't involved. There are two million people on Tercet—and she doesn't even have the technology to get off the ground, let alone pose a threat to the Regnum.''

"What would you have done if the Seers and I were still there?"

Hal didn't speak at first, nor did he turn around, but Bolla could see his shoulders squaring with some kind of determination—to speak the exact truth?

"I still wake up at night sometimes. When I do, I don't get back to sleep until I convince myself that I would have stuffed the captain down the officers' head and joined you.''

Bolla noted that Tyrees seemed to be having trouble with his contact lenses again. He was blinking and pinching the bridge of his nose.

"Dr. Bolla. Instruct the CP as soon as we return to *Condor*. Officer Ttig is to be reinstated to Cadre One.''

"Of course.''

As if a great weight had suddenly been lifted from them, the massive shoulders drooped forward. Before anything more could be said, a muted beep came from the car's dashboard. Hal touched a button.

"Hal. Code Five—send.''

A clear voice came over the car speakers. "FSO dispatcher, sir. Priority One. Singletary has breached the Council Order to close down off-planet traffic. Council messaged for instructions. Please acknowledge.''

"Acknowledged. Stand by.''

"Damn it!'' said Bolla. He felt a flush of heat pass through his chest. "Could Singletary have something to do with our Seer, Hal? This is the first time any government has directly disobeyed an Order in Council.''

Hal thought a moment. "I don't know, sir. Singletary is nominally a democracy—a regency, they call it—but Monoman, the Regent, functions more like a monarch. He does a lot of public bitching about the new regime. The field-support office here has been keeping a close watch on him, but there's been nothing blatant like this. Do you think he has anything to do with Las-trom's illness? Is that why you're here?''

"I doubt there's a connection," said Tyrees. "We'll visit the Seer before dealing with Monoman." His voice had the softness of a purring cat, and his expression was as placid. Bolla had learned to recognize the times when Tyrees had shifted into this mode. They were bad times.

"Here we are," said Hal.

The lead ground car was pulling over to a stop near a low stone wall, a curious anomaly in this very modern city. The separate stones were similar in origin, each bearing the same waved and gold-toned graining, like roughened wood, though they were irregular in shape. It was obviously built by hand, long ago when some patient craftsman was indifferent to the time it might take to build. Squashed between two towering structures of plasteel, the wall circled a stubborn compound containing a small, two-story house of the same stone. Another Cadre Four was waving their car through the narrow archway into the compound.

The house looked like that of a simple, perhaps prosperous, farmer. Hal was speaking as they stopped at its entrance.

"Las-trom was more than a little indignant when we descended upon him, but he cooperated. I can tell you that no one—*no one*—outside of the household came near him before he fell ill. The Cadre physician has been here ever since, but he can't give us a diagnosis except for 'accelerating neural dysfunction.' "

Hal led them quickly inside and down a dim hallway to an old, carved door, where he stood aside. Tyrees moved by him, but with a sharp intake of breath stopped abruptly before the door. He closed his eyes and his face contracted—as one might upon finding the rotting corpse of a rat in a just opened food container.

"Paghh!" He spat on the floor.

"What is it, Pol?"

"You can't smell the stench? . . . No, of course you can't."

Tyrees hesitated briefly, then opened the door. The room was clean and virtually bare, containing only a small desk and chair and a narrow cot. Some medical equipment, looking incongruously out of time and place, cluttered the desktop. The Seer, Las-trom, lay inert upon the cot under a thin blanket. Hollow cheeked and rice-paper pale, his face was moribund. One skeletal arm lay along his side, its elbow like a knot in a rope.

Tyrees walked slowly into the room a step at a time, each one an effort, as if he were wading into a swamp. He stood motionless over the figure on the cot for a long time. Finally, Bolla and Hal joined him. They could see Las-trom's breathing now—light and shallow—a leaf falling.

"What is it, Pol?" asked Bolla.

Without taking his eyes from the wasted body beneath him, Tyrees spoke in a halting whisper that somehow carried revulsion and awe—and perhaps fear—simultaneously.

"He has *been* here. I can feel him."

"No one has been in this house except Cadre personnel since he was under guard," said Hal. "No one."

Perspiration was forming on Tyrees's forehead. "And the surrounding area?"

"After he fell ill and we received the CP's instructions, the area was swept clean within a hundred-meter radius."

"You were probably too late—but Las-trom's still alive," muttered Tyrees. "I don't understand. . . ." Suddenly he reached to undo his collar clasp and let his cape fall to the floor. He bent over Las-trom, fingers probing on both sides of his head where the jawlines ended beneath the ears.

"Pol—"

"Be quiet, please."

Hal and Bolla looked at one another. Hal's expression was one of confusion; Bolla's was desperate. Tyrees had closed his eyes. Immediately his face contracted again into the pinched lines of something close to nausea. His throat caught—once, twice, three times—like a man fighting a vomit reflex. Then the spasms quieted and he seemed to gain a kind of control, even though the terrain of his brow melted from revulsion to pain, and finally to intense bewilderment.

Bolla remembered Shaamlik and had to fight an impulse to

throw himself at Tyrees. He caught a tremor in Las-trom's lips, and grabbed at Hal's arm.

"Oooohhhhh." The low, agonized moan came from the quavering mouth of the Seer. "Oooohhhh." One of the stick-thin arms lifted slowly and fell. "Oooohhhh."

"He's reviving!" gasped Hal.

And so it seemed to Bolla too—until he noticed that the moans were in cadence with an empty shaping of Tyrees's own lips.

"That's enough, Pol," he said, barely aware of the sound of his words. "That's enough!" He plunged at Tyrees, knocking the sturdy Hal backward like an unhinged gate. Growling, wrapping bearish arms around Tyrees, he tore him from the Seer with a violence he didn't know he possessed.

Tyrees hung slack in Bolla's grip for a time, his arms pinned to his sides. Bolla himself was breathing in heavy rasps. He could feel his heart racing perilously, and might have fallen if a confused Hal had not begun to peel his arms away, supporting them both.

"Calm yourself, Hans. I'm all right. Calm yourself." Tyrees's voice brought him out of his near faint.

"I wasn't . . . going to let you . . . to let you . . ."

"I know. Sit down—here." A chair was dragged under him and he slumped into it. "I was in no danger, Hans. Calm yourself now." Tyrees let a fingertip linger on an artery in Bolla's neck. He nodded at Hal, frowned, then smiled.

"You're too old and fat, Doctor, for such behavior. Rest. Breathe deeply."

"You'll—you'll kill me yet, you—you goddamn . . ."

A lightning stroke of fear shot over Tyrees's face—so quickly that Hal wasn't sure it had struck.

"Nobody can kill you, you old reprobate. But thank you. Breaking contact would have been difficult—and draining. You saved me time. We have serious problems to deal with."

Bolla began to breathe easier. He looked up at Tyrees and rubbed the frizz of hair on his pate.

"Okay. Tell us what's wrong with Las-trom. What are we dealing with?"

Tyrees looked at the body on the cot. He moved to replace the arm that had fallen and was hanging stiffly off the edge. He spoke as if each word were brittle, not to be uttered carelessly.

"He's . . . like a fetus, Doctor. There is *nothing* there. No memories, no awareness of self. Nothing. Murder isn't the right word for it. It was . . . rape of a kind, only worse. Violation. A horrible violation, because he must have known it was happening."

Blood rose into Hal's face. "I told you, Pol—no one came *near* this man!"

"It appears that he didn't have to," said Tyrees. "It's not your fault, Ttig." His voice had taken on a subtle, haunted chord that layered almost soundlessly with the others. Bolla, uncertain he had detected it, wished Radis were there. "It's worse than I thought, Doctor. The Seer's mind was *wiped*— wiped clean!"

Bolla felt bile rise in his stomach. "Will he live? I mean, if he isn't damaged physically . . ."

"He is. The body and the mind are only separate in stupid philosophies, Hans. The man's mind is a network of hollow tunnels now. The body gets no . . . direction. It's degenerating. Even the autonomic system is failing."

"It *must* be a Seer, then. The maverick."

"Yes. Or something worse that I can't imagine. . . . I have difficulty imagining *this!*" He looked one more time at the length of mindless tissue on the cot. "He did this to a Tercian Seer," he muttered, half to himself. "Like a wave washing over writing in the sand."

"What?"

"There's nothing to stop him, Hans. In time he can destroy them all. All the Seers."

Bolla was shocked. These were not the words of the man who refused to stop until he held the destiny of a galaxy in the palm of his hand.

"That's foolishness, Pol. You're tired. We've lost only three

Seers. We have the resources of the Regnum at our disposal."

Tyrees smiled—almost evilly. "As I said before, Hans. That's what the Chairman thought. Now he's mindless too."

"We will find him," hissed Bolla, jowls trembling, "and we will excise him, cut him out like a tumor."

Tyrees raised his eyebrows in surprise, not knowing that Bolla's uncharacteristic bloody-mindedness had arisen out of his leader's despond.

"And how do we do that? How do we get *close* to him? Locate him on a planet—this one perhaps—and blow it to hell? The Chairman and Tercet again?"

Bolla shrugged, feigning nonchalance after his outburst. "Of course not, *Vitar. You* will deal with him. He can not possibly have your—"

"Listen to me!" The three words were an explosion of anger. Bolla instinctively fell back a step. Hal's hands fingered the edges of his cape nervously. *"Accept a fact! If that man were standing here now, I would be there!"* Tyrees jerked his head at the cot.

"You don't know that," said Bolla softly, though his stomach was now a ball of writhing things. "Meta-sol always said that no man knew what you could do—including yourself."

This time the evocation of that name had no effect. Tyrees whirled on his heel and threw open the door. Bolla and the thoroughly confused Ttig Hal followed.

When the three burst from the main entrance, they were greeted by a semicircle of aimed and waiting lasguns.

Seven

Can ye vanquish the enemy without knowing him? Can ye know
without sharing his darkness? Can ye share his darkness with
being claimed?

—The Te

BOLLA WAS THE last out. He was one second later in taking
the ring of weapons, the bodies of the Cadre surveillance te
on the ground, the gray uniforms of the Singletary Guard.
scene had just formed in his mind when Hal's voice roa
out.

"What the *hell* is this!"

There were five of them—four leveling the lasguns, and
with maroon flashes on his chest standing to one side. He
the one who spoke.

"You are under arrest. Step closer and lie facedown on
ground."

"The *hell* you say!" Under the umbrella of Hal's outra
Bolla did not feel the danger of the weapons. "You can
we're Cadre, man! You have no authority over us! I
personally have your head for this!" He was pointing at
nearest Number Four, who was crumpled into a fetal positio
few feet away.

The Singletary officer hesitated, but answered calmly.

have the authority of the personal order of the Regent of Singletary.''

"*He* has no authority. You are committing a serious crime, mister. Your Regent is breaking Regnum law. . . .''

"My orders are to kill, if you resist arrest!'' shrieked the officer. His calm had vanished, but not his determination. "Lie on the ground!''

Bolla saw Tyrees's knees bend slowly, his arms reaching downward as if to follow the order. Then he sprang. No animal, no jungle cat could have matched the speed or the power of that leap. Bolla caught the most fleeting of images: Tyrees, neck high and parallel to the ground, the length of his body whipping over the lasguns and into three of the men before they could register the motion, let alone increase pressure on trigger fingers. A sophisticated camera would have recorded the simultaneous action: Tyrees's knee axing into the temple of one; his elbow impacting into the lower jaw of another; the middle row of knuckles on one fist spearing into the throat of the third. The first two, having bones shattered, were unconscious before they hit the ground. The third was dead.

As the fourth man was swinging his lasgun toward the mayhem, Tyrees was already rising to his feet. By then Hal was in motion. His kick to the solar plexus lifted the man off the ground. He writhed when he landed, struggling for breath until he blacked out.

The officer had had time only to back off two steps farther. His face was grotesque with fear. "Fire!'' he screamed. "Fire!''

From the low stone wall came innocuous hums, bee buzzes that reformed quickly into one ominous pulse. Tyrees and Hal folded like spineless dolls onto the walkway.

Through it all Bolla had stood immobile, one hand trembling on the rough stone of the entrance archway. A wave of heat which he felt as shame—shame for his obesity and his paralyzing fear—passed over his cheeks and brow. He raised his other hand and with butterfly fingers fluttered at a sudden sting in his eyes—the salt of tears or sweat—which he couldn't identify. The scene before him was the stuff of cheap and easy fiction arranged to appeal to the buried savagery of the masses of doltish holovision watchers. Bodies everywhere, some touching, crumpled into unlikely positions and displaying no blood. Tyrees's and Hal's capes were one black shroud placed with tasteless calculation to simulate an effect of finality and romance. The officer didn't fit the scene: he was too real, the muscles of his face ajump, his lips soundless but moving as he struggled with the realization that he was unharmed and in control. Three armed men, their invisible strings having been pulled, rose like puppets from behind the stone wall.

Without volition, Bolla staggered forward.

"Stop!"

He stared at the officer stupidly.

"Stay as you are." The officer had regained composure and stepped partway through the bodies. "You are Bolla, the Vitar's man? The Chairman of the Regnum Council?"

He said nothing, because he had no will to speak. He blinked at the bite in his eyes. The officer stepped over more bodies— very daintily, it seemed to Bolla—and stopped in front of him. A smile broke on the man's face—a radiant smile, as if he had just come to a full awareness of his vitality and his freedom. Casually, he brought one arm across his chest and rested his hand for a moment on his shoulder. Still smiling, still casual, he swung a backhanded slash into Bolla's face.

"Answer me."

Bolla reeled, more from shock than pain. He was a small child when he had last been struck—a smack on the bottom by an irritated parent. This was . . . humiliating, outrageous, appalling, cosmic in its injustice. It was an overwhelming experience, totally new and debilitating, and it obliterated even the knowledge of the carnage around him. He welcomed it. Blood trickled from his nose. He could taste it. He welcomed that, too, even as his shaking fingers wiped at it. Somehow, it made him more whole.

From one of the men Tyrees had downed came a small whimper. Bolla drew himself up.

"You have no idea," he said with dignity, "what you have done here." He looked at the draped figure of Tyrees.

The officer smirked. He was still amazed, drugged by a sense of invulnerability. "The Cadre men are still alive. Our weapons were set for stun. We couldn't take the risk of killing *you*, could we?"

Bolla caught his breath, felt his heart seize. He waited in fearful joy for it to resume pumping.

"Why . . . why have you done this?"

"Answer *my* question, old man. Are you Bolla?"

"You know that I am. What you *don't* know is just how serious is the thing you have done here."

The officer's smile faltered somewhat. "I follow my Regent's orders. He's not frightened by religious fanatics—and neither am I."

He turned and stooped to pull a lasgun from under the guardsman who was still mewing softly, jerking in spasms as if he were sleeping fitfully under the spell of a bad dream. The officer's smile returned. With careful ostentation he lifted the weapon and displayed it to Bolla. An audible click sounded as he pulled a recessed lever. Delicately, he used a booted foot to nudge Hal's cape aside.

"Purple collar. Cadre Two, isn't it?"

Bolla remained silent—and desperate. His hard-won courage evaporated in a hot, rushing wind—another new awareness: his unctuous, naive words had tipped him toward catastrophe. It was horribly ridiculous. He was a psychologist. He should know. This was a simple soldier here, holding a killing weapon. The man had just emerged the fortuitous victor in a deadly contest. The efficacy of that victory had just been impugned. What could the adrenaline-soaked man be expected to do?

Using his boot toe again, the officer tugged at Hal's head, turning it face up. Bolla could hear the soft sound as flesh abraided with stone.

"No. Please. No."

The officer lowered the lasgun to within centimeters of Hal's forehead.

"I'm sure the Vitar's lackey and a Cadre One will be more than enough for the Regent."

Bolla pleaded, "Don't . . . please." His nose and throat filled with phlegm and he started to choke.

The officer pulled the trigger. A small black hole formed on Hal's forehead. There was a very small wisp of smoke.

Eight

Death itself seems acceptable. It fits the scheme of things as we see them—everything becomes compost. But if we do accept it, then consciousness *is not acceptable.*

—The Sayings of Meta-sol

BOLLA FELT RANK. He could smell himself. He had extra folds in his flesh where things unpleasant could collect, and he was very aware of it. Even a few hours without access to washing facilities would always set his nerves on edge.

He watched Tyrees squirm. It was a sign of returning consciousness, and that was good. But these were the writhings—slow and yet spasmodic—of nightmare. Odd sounds came from his lips. Some were probably words, but most were more primal and defensive, the quiet snarls and whimpers of a dog waiting for the whip.

Bolla stretched his jaw and rubbed the faintly irritated flesh of his neck. The room was quite luxurious, more befitting an expensive tourist haven than a prison. Tasteful prints adorned the walls, comfortable furniture blended well with the decor. The absence of windows might go unnoticed because of the fine drapes. Even the fabric bindings that shackled Tyrees's wrists to the arms of his reclined lounger were unobtrusive.

Bolla was tired, his nerves strung out and fraying, but he was still morbidly fascinated with the twitchings of the body across from him. No one knew better than he that the mind trapped in that body had a horror of the inchoate, of the loss of control, and that that mind contained a will that demanded diamond-hard perfection. Yet at this time it and its body were the playthings of . . . of what? Random electrochemical activity? Dark dreams imaged on the walls of cells that recalled the bruitish plunge of birth?

"Pol . . . Pol, can you hear me?"

The spasms and the sounds continued, but seemed to abate somewhat.

Bolla sighed and closed his own eyes, trying to absorb the fatigue by relaxing, for he knew he couldn't sleep. As he stared into the darkness behind his eyelids, an old, familiar anxiety nudged closer to the surface. Every month now, it seemed, it rose higher, pushed harder. He tried to listen to the sluggish ball of his heart buried beneath his superfluity of flesh, imagined it struggling absurdly against a tide of time and abuse. He wished he had devoted himself to the Learning instead of politics and power. Or would that only have increased the anxiety?

"Where are we, Hans?"

Bolla knew that Tyrees's recovery would come quickly, but he was still surprised. Tyrees was looking at him expectantly. He had just regained consciousness to find himself a prisoner, bound and in the hands of an enemy with unknown designs. Only the Maker knew what was hanging in the balance, and this man had put his question in the same manner as another would ask the time.

"I don't know. Are you all right?"

Tyrees nodded. "Yes. A bit woolly, though. They got us with stun set?"

"They did indeed."

Tyrees looked around him. "A rather well-appointed dungeon. We are close to power, in any case."

"No doubt." Bolla rolled his eyes upward and across the ceiling. "No doubt our hosts will be paying us a visit soon."

"No, Hans," said Tyrees, having caught the signal. "We're not being monitored. Probably because they know we would expect to be and didn't bother. I don't think they're after information anyway."

Bolla took for granted the accuracy of Tyrees's assertion that they could speak safely. "You're probably right. It seems they were after *me*, in any case. They don't know your identity, Pol."

Tyrees thought for a moment. "They couldn't have known we were coming, so it must have been a snap decision made when we—you—were recognized after landfall."

"That seems likely," agreed Bolla, "but something was already brewing, or they wouldn't have taken such a drastic step. Singletary has not been satisfied with her lack of privilege since the coup." He produced an elephantine handkerchief from a slash pocket of his gown and proceeded to mop at his jowls. "Do you think there is any connection between Singletary and the Seer deaths?"

"No." Tyrees let himself fall back on the lounger as if he would have preferred to leave the question unanswered. He rolled his head toward Bolla. "In that case we would have been attacked by . . . less conventional weapons."

Bolla nodded. He stared at the gray eyes for the thousandth time, for the thousandth time obscurely glad that a film of plastic lay between him and the real eyes. Even with that shield, he could see them flare as the head with the unfamiliar brown hair lifted an inch. He waited for the inevitable question.

"Ttig. Where is Ttig?"

Bolla spread his handkerchief on his lap, folding it carefully, gathering together, husbanding, a few more seconds.

"He's dead, Pol. That officer killed him."

"Why?" The single word was softly spoken—and vast. A chasm opening. Bolla could only shake his head. *"Why?"*

"Because . . . it was a fit of pique. No more, I think. I was stupid, Pol. The man was . . . hyped up, and I challenged him, threatened him. I should have kept my foolish mouth shut."

Tyrees let himself settle back slowly into the lounger. He seemed to shrink into it, his head turning to the wall. Bolla could hear his heart now, in the silence. It was a clock of mushy flesh and it counted the seconds slowly, grudgingly, only because it had to.

"I'm sorry, Pol." Bolla blew noisily into his folded square of cloth.

"So am I." Tyrees's words bounced gently off the wall near his face before coming to Bolla. "Another sacrifice."

"Pol, don't be—"

"I know. People have to die. But why do I have to kill them? Why do they have to die for *me?* Stay away from me, Doctor. I kill everyone I touch."

Nine

Life is bracketed pain.

—The Teraac

THE REGENT'S CHAMBERS were opulent, rich with the products of the artisan's hands and his imagination. Along every wall recessed alcoves contained sculptures—some on pedestals, some free standing—all of the same shell-white stone, a delicately veined, soft-seeming substance that accepted well the voluptuous curve and the imitation of flesh. The figures, mostly nudes, had a buttery sheen as if they were lightly oiled, and they begged for the touch of a hand. Their poses were blatantly sensual, inviting, narcissistic celebrations of beauty and pleasure. Only the restraint of the stone kept them from exaggeration: breasts were oversized and thrusting, loins open, arms casually beckoning. The handsome faces, male and female, all possessed or promised indulgence. Lips pursed with lightly reined desire, or smiled ripeful and unsated.

Ornately draped paintings occupied the spaces between the alcoves, bringing a contrast of rich color to the sculptures. These were extravagant scenes of feasters at laden tables, lovers reclined and laughing, daubing at wine on their chins. One depicted an elderly, aristocratic man with lush red cheeks and half-lidded eyes, languishing in a canopied bed. He was lifting the stopper from a jeweled vial for a cherubic young boy who was leaning forward to inhale. The vial held him in thrall.

Pol Tyrees sat, half sunken, in a plush, golden divan. With his stark Cadre uniform and his hard, ascetic face, he gave the impression of a black spider having come to rest upon a royal sleeve. Bound at the wrists, his hands lay quietly in his lap. Bolla sat opposite him in an identical divan, his soft bulk more befitting its comfortable luxury, his expression concerned, but more accepting, more compromising, for he was now operating on his terrain—words. Nevertheless, he was fidgeting with his handkerchief.

The Regent sat in state in a high-backed, wide-winged chair—the focus of the large room because of its position and size. He was a large man with an impressive bearing. Heavy jewels sparked complacently on heavy fingers. Thick dark hair, waved with silver, undulated around his face and curved back over his ears. A slight puffiness of flesh, a tinge of floridness in the skin, a hint of hidden flab under the rich, purple gown suggested an induced, premature middle age. His name was Monoman, and he spoke with the assurance of a man long accustomed to speaking from a position of strength.

"My demands are clear, are they not? You will simply verify them in a message to your Vitar." He was speaking to Bolla, ignoring Tyrees. "Singletary must have total autonomy."

Bolla was refolding his gargantuan handkerchief. "You have that already, Regent."

Monoman smiled, revealing glossy white, sightly uneven teeth. "Please. You are not in a position to play stupid games. Our autonomy must be extended beyond Singletary's orbiting circle. We will trade with whomever we please, in whatever commodities we please, under whatever conditions we please."

Bolla returned the smile. "You may have those things very easily. Secede. The Regnum does not force membership."

"And then, of course, we would be squeezed out." The Regent raised a tight fist. "We would be free only to deal with a few paupers—the nonmember planets."

"You ask to be given a special status that no other member of the Regnum enjoys. Your present prosperity is the result of illegal arrangements with the former Chairman. Accept that advantage from history and be satisfied. The old regime is dead."

The Regent's shoulders rose and pressed back into his chair. He had not expected such incautious rebuke from the fat old man. "Regardless of your interpretation of history, we demand what is ours by precedent."

"And my freedom, you think, will buy the Council's agreement?" Bolla chuckled as if this were an impossibility.

"Not at all. You err on two points." The Regent paused for effect, reaching for and sipping from an exquisite goblet containing a bright red liquid. "It is not the Council's agreement we seek—its members are puppets. We will accept only the Vitar's *public* word. We will 'buy' that word, not with your freedom, but with your *life,* Dr. Bolla."

Bolla felt pain rise into his chest, but he managed to betray no sign of it. The casual, almost offhand manner of the Regent's threat left him breathless, but his negotiator's instincts took over, and he took refuge in them. It would at least give him time to reorder his thoughts. He dare not even glance in Tyrees's direction.

"Your gamble is outrageously dangerous, Regent. One taken on the spur of the moment, since my visit was impromptu. I cannot guarantee the Vitar's response, but I do know this: I would rather die than bear the brunt of his anger."

The Regent's aristocratic brow furrowed with affront. "His anger is a matter of utter indifference to me. Unlike the fanatics of the New Covenant—some of whom I have hitherto allowed to fester freely on Singletary—I am aware of the fact that he is *just another man.*"

Bolla stared unblinkingly at him for a long time. _"That,"_ he said softly, "is a great flaw in your awareness." He shook his head, as if in exasperation over an incredible folly. "You've gone almost too far already, but I think I can concede you this: you acted precipitately, out of misunderstanding; my sudden appearance on Singletary confused you; I will intercede with the Vitar on your behalf. That is all I can offer you."

The Regent froze for a moment. Were he washed of color, he would have been a fitting addition to his own collection of statuary. Then his moist lips curled, and with a swipe of his arm he snatched up the goblet again, rings clicking against the crystal, and he quaffed the drink in one swallow. As the goblet came away from his mouth he was laughing heartily. Tiny reddish bubbles foamed on his teeth. A servant appeared with a decanter, but he had to make several attempts before the goblet came to rest in the Regent's hand long enough to pour the scarlet substance.

When the laughter subsided, an invisible wand passed over the Regent's face—puffing it, flushing it, carving out of it unguarded, natural lines of decadence. Doubt was not a thing that lingered long on such a countenance.

"You are the prisoner here," he said. "You have _nothing_ to offer me." He tilted his head to one side, looking at Bolla quizzically. "But you can satisfy my curiosity. Why should the Council's watchdog 'suddenly appear' on Singletary? And why with such a high-ranking Cadre robot in tow?"

For the first time Tyrees spoke. "We came because—"

"Be silent," cut in the Regent. "You'll be told, if you're required to speak." He glared at the black figure slouched into the golden divan as he would at a stain of grease. "You are here and breathing only because you _may_ be convenient as a messenger."

Bolla spoke quickly, drawing Monoman's attention away from Tyrees. "You were not informed because my visit was not a matter of state. The Seer, Las-trom is dying. He is an old friend of the Vitar's—and mine. I came to offer our respects.

This Cadre One''—he nodded at Tyrees—''is my body-guard.''

Monoman snorted. ''A Cadre One for a bodyguard? Isn't that a waste of his talents?''

''He can be put to use in many ways,'' said Bolla deliberately cryptical.

''I can understand the Vitar's right-hand man having his privileges, but why was your Seer so heavily guarded?''

Tyrees spoke for the second time, now with obvious contempt in his voice. ''We suspected foul play, *Regent*. We are well aware of Singletary's treacherous leanings.''

Monoman's goblet stopped halfway to his lips. ''I told you to keep your silence. You irritate me.'' He jerked his head and an armed man in the ubiquitous uniform of the Singletary Guard appeared instantly. It was the same officer who had confronted them at the door of the Seer.

''Tell these gentlemen your orders, Major.''

''Yes, Regent.'' He nodded in Tyrees's direction. ''To kill this man if he so much as attempts to rise.''

Tyrees chuckled softly, cruelly, like a man tormenting an angry puppy. He snapped up the tether that secured his bound wrists to a leg of the divan. ''How can I rise with this?''

A bolt of fear passed over the officer's face. ''This man is extremely dangerous, Regent.''

''So you have told me, Major,'' said Monoman, sipping, ''but he is harmless enough now. At the moment it is his impertinence that concerns me.''

''Would it be impertinent if I called you and your lackey murderers?'' Even more than the words themselves, something in the quality of Tyrees's voice alarmed the Regent. He set his goblet down with exaggerated care and pulled himself to his feet. Three steps brought him to tower over Tyrees. The major moved quickly to a position behind the divan.

''Regent!'' sputtered Bolla, ''You cannot—''

''There will be no more diplomacy!'' roared Monoman. He stabbed a bejeweled finger to within centimeters of Tyrees's forehead. "Tell me why you came to Singletary!"

The major grabbed Tyrees's hair and jerked his head back viciously. There was a soft tearing sound as the adhesive gave and part of the wig came away. The look that passed between Monoman and the officer was only startled at first; then the Regent's mouth fell open when he took a closer look at Tyrees. Swearing softly, he reached out a less than steady hand and tore the wig completely away.

"The Vitar," he breathed, stepping back. "It's the Vitar."

Bolla unfolded his handkerchief, sighed, and rolled his eyes to the heavens. Tyrees smiled.

"Now that you have me, Regent, what are you going to *do* with me?"

Staring, Monoman began to twist absently at his rings. He backed to his chair without taking his eyes from Tyrees and eased himself slowly into it. One hand groped for the goblet and slowly brought it to his lips. It came away empty. The servant returned, frightened, skipping like a man on hot coals. He had trouble controlling the decanter while pouring, and some of the red liquid spilled on the Regent's hand. He didn't notice.

Monoman looked at the major. "Leave us."

"But Regent—"

"Leave us!" The major saluted and started away. "No—wait!" The finger that pointed at Tyrees earlier was now aimed at the officer. The man's face was a canvas, and on it was painted the fact that he had been through too much that day. "Gather together those who have seen this, and impress upon them how much their lives depend upon their silence. Then—all of you—remain out of earshot."

"Yes, Regent."

When he had gone, Monoman sat for a long time sipping from his goblet, staring. Tyrees ducked his head to his bound hands to remove the lenses from his eyes. When he looked up again, the Regent started slightly, as if from the sting of an insect. The eyes glared at him like blue suns upon tender white flesh.

Bolla spoke first. "You can't contain the Vitar, Regent. He's too big for you."

Monoman moistened his heavy lips. "I can destroy him."

"Can you?" Bolla asked the question as if it were an interesting but doubtful premise.

"He's only a man—only a man."

"Is he?" Bolla paused, letting the Regent think of the unthinkable. "Assuming you could, what would happen then? Allow me to speculate." Almost enjoying himself now, Bolla steepled his chubby fingers in his best professorial manner. "Even here, on Singletary, the followers of the New Covenant would be screaming for your blood. That is to say nothing of the rest of the Regnum. You couldn't survive it. The Vitar is too big for you, Regent."

Monoman's face grew florid. His thick fingers grew restless on the goblet. "There would be many who would follow me," he said. "And the gullible zealots who consider him a god would be disillusioned. His executioner would be a man to be feared."

Bolla shook his head sadly. "You are a fool. You think what you want to think."

"You have too much concern for his welfare, Dr. Bolla." The light flared off Tyrees's naked skull as he let his head fall negligently to the back of the divan. He looked at the Regent from under indolent, half-lidded, deadly eyes.

Monoman took a hurried swallow from the goblet. A red dribble collected in the crease of his chin.

"Why did you come to Singletary?"

"To see *you*," said Tyrees. "To judge your fitness to rule. I have already made that judgment."

The Regent laughed a falsetto laugh. Bolla saw sweat appear along the line formed on the Regent's brow by his silvery hair. Tyrees was going too far, he thought, but the goading seemed to be intentional. What was he after?

Monoman was on his feet again. "You are my prisoner, tin god!" he screamed. "I sit in judgment over *you!*" With a grand sweep of his arm he flung a wet swath from his goblet across Tyrees's chest. The red slash on the Cadre uniform looked like a mortal sword wound.

Tyrees didn't even blink. "Some judge, some ruler," he said scornfully. "That is the action of a self-indulgent, foolish, and *cowardly* old man."

Monoman's lips pulled back from his teeth with a cat's venomous hiss, and he flung the heavy goblet with savage accuracy at Tyrees's head. The missile had barely two meters to travel to its target—but Tyrees's head was suddenly to one side, as if it had always been there. The goblet sailed over the divan and shattered on the polished floor, its fragments skittering the full length of the room.

Tyrees smirked. "And you have the impotent temper of a child. You are not fit to rule."

Now the hiss was so wild, something released from such deep, primal rage, that spittle flew from between Monoman's teeth as he lunged. Bolla felt pain jump into his chest, and his cry was as much a response to it as the attack. Monoman's heavy, beringed fingers, jewels sparking violently, were around Tyrees's throat. The hiss stopped abruptly as Bolla was struggling to his feet. Monoman could feel his hands being forced minutely back by neck muscles tautening like metal cables. He curled the ends of his fingers, trying to dig them into the softer flesh even as his rage was dying and fear was rising to take its place.

Before the running figure of the major could reach them— even before Bolla could—the feral expression on the Regent's face had changed to one of utter incredulity. His eyes were wide and bulging, his chin trembling.

Bolla stopped. It seemed now as if Monoman were actually trying to let go, trying to scream, but he could not. Bolla watched the pupils of his eyes roll sickeningly upward and disappear. The major arrived, bringing his weapon to bare just as his Regent was toppling to the floor. He fell of a piece, rigidly, like one of his own statues, tipped. The blunt spear of Tyrees's boot toe caught the major in the throat. There was the dull, flat sound of a bone breaking when he went down. The bone belonged to Monoman, because his elbow joint, a thing of plaster now, refused to bend naturally when it took the major's weight.

Bolla stood there, aghast. Waves of strange sensation passed over him, drenching his armpits, making him dizzy. How wonderful the relief, how gratifying the revenge, how terrible the killing power of the Vitar.

With trembling hands he rolled his sodden square of cloth into a ball and summoned his voice. "Bring your Vicc-Regent!" he croaked. There were sounds of frightened voices and scurrying feet.

Tyrees had sprawled back into the divan, breathing heavily, sapped. His face was ashen, his eyes glazed over as they were when he was sighting for the pathways. His bound wrists quivered slightly. He was murmuring something. Bolla leaned closer.

"Must touch me . . . get him to touch me . . ."

"What? What are you saying, Pol?"

"Can't . . . can't do what *he* does . . . kill him . . . try to *kill* him . . ."

Bolla looked down at the Regent. He was still breathing, his chest heaving convulsively, though the rest of his body was catatonic. So Tyrees had not been able to kill him. It came to Bolla with horrible certainty that Tyrees had been trying to match the destructive powers of the murderer they pursued! And he had failed. What had been foremost in his mind—the Mephistophelian experiment, or the saving of their lives? Now he knew what it was that Meta-sol had feared in Pol-Nesol-Rast, Seer of the Gathering.

Ten

To seek and not to yield? Does that mean to seek and destroy?

—The Sayings of Meta-sol

ONCE MORE *CONDOR* rode a great updraft into the Void. She was not at home, here on the pathway. Space was her home, the dimension of her thriving, but this was not space. This was a dark tunnel plunging through it, confining, directing, alien. Its existence was rendered only through the washed and murky child's smear of colors on the bridge screen.

Tyrees rose from the command chair with less difficulty, it seemed to Bolla, than he had on the flight to Singletary.

"Take the chair, Captain."

Again Bolla followed him—uninvited—to his quarters. There were questions that had to be asked.

When Tyrees was seated before his console, he surprised Bolla by asking a question of his own. "Hans, when was the last time you had a medical?"

"Why? I am in perfect health."

Tyrees looked at him. Islands of ice fired with blue looked at him from the bottom of dark caverns.

"It's strange that a man who watches *me* so closely, who is always so concerned about *my* health, is so neglectful of his own.''

Bolla chuckled. He patted his stomach fondly, as if it were something detached from him, like a favorite pet. ''Let the old man be, Pol. Do as I do—indulge him because he's still alive after all these years. *You're* still young, but you're using yourself up faster than I am.''

''Would that you were wise before you were old,'' said Tyrees, turning away to the console.

''Hah! I do believe the youthful master of the universe is lecturing the old man with quotations! Such presumption. I am shocked.'' Bolla waggled his head and gave way to his famous, huffing laugh, but he was continuing before Tyrees could say more. ''Your function is to listen to *me*. Mine is to guide you. Nature planned it that way, my boy, and she's a lot wiser than either of us.''

Tyrees tapped at the keys before him, but his screen remained blank. Bolla wondered idly what impulse would prompt him, what message he would send into a dead machine. What made a man write some words just to put them in a bottle and toss them into the sea?

''Very well, Doctor. Nature has it that the young are not permitted to guide the old. But what if age is *wrong?* What then?''

Bolla sobered instantly. He looked at the back of Tyrees's gleaming skull.

''Perhaps that is our most important lesson. That we, too, are fallible.'' Tyrees turned around. ''You've been very fortunate, Pol. You've had many . . . fathers. But I am the last.'' Bolla smiled. ''So it goes without saying that I should be cherished.''

Tyrees smiled also. ''What is the lesson for today, Hans? I have a feeling that neither of us is ready to accept your fallibility yet.''

''You see? You *are* gaining wisdom,'' sighed Bolla with feigned fatigue. Actually he was feeling rejuvenated after his sleep and a long, hot shower. He produced a crisp, new handkerchief, large enough to serve as the cloth for a small table. "No lesson. Just a little chat. Radis would call it a 'debriefing.' "

Tyrees shook his head. "Inaccurate, Doctor, if you're referring to Singletary. A Cadre debriefer seeks information when an officer returns from the field. You were there yourself."

"Don't quibble. Just answer a few questions. First—why didn't you use *Condor* as a threat? You left the captain with appropriate instructions."

Tyrees reached for Meta-sol's cane and placed it gently in his lap. "I intended to—until Monoman discovered who I was. He would have called the bluff."

Bolla puffed out his cheeks. "Okay, that sounds reasonable. But why did you deliberately inflame him? You couldn't predict what he would do."

Tyrees caressed the smooth cane tenderly with his slender fingers. "Yes, I could. He's an easy man to read—I could read his whole life's story on his face. And I wanted him to touch me."

"You wanted him to touch you so you could see what you could *do* to him," said Bolla quietly.

Tyrees's fingers curled around the cane tightly. "Yes."

Bolla's voice grew even quieter. "A rather . . . macabre bit of experimentation, is it not, Pol?"

The hard blue eyes narrowed. "It suited my purposes."

"Against the maverick Seer or the Regent?"

"Both."

"You would have killed the Regent—if you could."

"Yes. Just like he killed Ttig. One more *sacrifice*." Tyrees thrust the cane back into its niche. "And how did you think we were going to get out of there?"

Bolla shrugged, keeping his eyes away from Tyrees, fixing them on his folding exercises. "I don't know . . . the time track, perhaps?"

"I told you I would never do that again."

Anger had slithered into Tyrees's voice. It was something that Bolla rarely heard and had never felt it aimed so directly at him, so he was surprised by its power. A poison spread through him, coursing with his blood. He realized that Tyrees sensed his shock, for the fangs were immediately withdrawn with his next words.

"I don't even know if I *can* do it now, Doctor. I don't want to know."

"But you wanted to know if you can do what our killer does."

Tyrees hesitated, but answered calmly. "It will come down to a contest," he said. "If we can find him."

"Come now, Pol!" Bolla was exasperated now. "You sound like a little boy with a tin shield and a wooden sword. A contest!" He flapped his cloth pettishly in the air before stuffing it away into an inner pocket of his gown.

"That's exactly right, Doctor. We never really become *men*. You know that—you've spent a lifetime studying the phenomenon. As we grow, we simply replace the last toy with a more sophisticated one. We grow, but we never grow *up*. We get stronger and smarter, but we never mature. Maturity is a cunning self-deception."

Bolla looked at him with only partly feigned amazement. "Really! And only a moment ago you were talking about age and wisdom!"

"Wisdom comes with a recognition of that fact—and an acceptance of it. We are much less than we suppose ourselves to be, Hans." Tyrees rubbed absently at the spot on his forehead where an eyebrow used to be. Bolla knew he was very tired, for his actions were seldom without deliberation.

"That's a rather cynical outlook, Pol. As a psychologist I am tempted to agree with you; but as a psychologist I can also say that even if it's true, it's not healthy."

"The truth is not *healthy?*"

"Quite often, as a matter of fact."

Tyrees smiled without mirth. "Well, the fact that I cannot *win* the little boy's contest which is to come doesn't augur well for *my* health."

Suddenly Bolla felt less concerned about the wreck of a man Tyrees had left back on Singletary. "It still doesn't have to come to that," he said. "The courts have an efficient way to dispose of murderers."

"I don't see this man being taken prisoner, Doctor, much less going through a trial."

"In that case his innards are no more impervious to laser burn than any other man's."

Tyrees spun his chair to the console. He stared at the blank face of its screen. "In that," he said, "you are doubtless correct. But the one with the gun had better be there without his knowledge—because no man alive could pull the trigger."

Eleven

When ye face the Maker, what will ye see? Will ye see a master of death? Will ye see a Vitar—a giver of life? Take care to decide if there is a difference. Take care that ye will not be gazing into the prophecy of a mirror.

—The Teraac

"ANOTHER SEER DIED a few hours ago."

Radis threw the hard copy upon the table as if he were dashing the head of a snake against rock. "It seems the Cadre is incapable of protecting them."

They sat in the balcony room atop the Citadel. Tyrees and Bolla had been back on Regnum only long enough for a change of clothes and a sample of their normal diet. Both had opportunity on the return trip aboard *Condor* for rest, but neither showed it. Tyrees was morose, thinner, his blue eyes burning like those of a man ravaged with fever, a fire banked and contained inside. Bolla's flaps and folds of flesh had loosened, changing a jolly figure into that of a melting Buddha. Radis, as discomfited by their lack of visible reaction as he was by his news, picked the copy up again.

"Sector Eight. Less than a year as a Seer. He fell over like a tree hit by lightning—*under the eyes of two Cadre officers.*"

Tyrees raised his eyes from the floor, but he looked at Bolla, not Radis. "Suggestion, Doctor?"

Bolla shook his head. His voice was flat. "I've stopped thinking about this as an aberration. I'm frightened now. I need more time to deal with it."

"Time!" exclaimed Radis. "In *time* he'll wipe out *all* the Seers. And long before that the public is going to be involved. There's going to be panic."

Bolla sighed. "It's 'let the great axe fall' is it?"

"If by that you mean I think it's time for drastic action, you are right. His advantages are anonymity and some very special abilities. The advantages we possess are political power and almost unlimited physical resources. The longer we delay in using them, the more they are diminished."

Radis was upon the firm ground of his extensive training and experience as a Cadre officer, so he spoke with assurance. His reading of the effects of the Singletary trip upon Bolla and the Vitar only hardened his opinion.

These things were not lost on Bolla. "You speak like a security expert, Radis."

"And how am I supposed to speak? I know I'm right." He looked to Tyrees for support, but the eyes were back on the floor. He had left them again. The debate had enlivened Bolla somewhat. The old, professorial tone was creeping back into his voice.

"In your own way you're a clever man, Radis, but like all young men, you disregard the most valuable teacher of all the disciplines."

"That being?"

"History."

"Oh shit." Radis tossed the hard copy at the table and collapsed into a chair.

"Precisely, 'Oh shit.' You have made an admirable effort— with the help of your Seer—and gained a measure of the capacity to meditate. That is splendid, even *surprising*, given the narrowness of the Cadre mentality. But meditation is not the same as *reflection*."

"Reflection? *Reflection?* What the hell does *that* mean? Is that something old men lay claim to because they can't do anything else?'' Radis smiled, somewhat ashamed of the insult, but not displeased by the color it summoned to Bolla's wan, full moon of a face.

''Crudely put, but not far from the mark,'' said Bolla after a moment's hesitation. ''When old men can't do anything else, they sometimes apply what is left of their senile minds to ponder the *important* questions.''

The smile left Radis's face. ''Don't patronize me, Dr. Bolla. And don't spew irrelevant philosophy at me in the middle of what is fast becoming a crisis. There is no question more important than the security of the Regnum.''

''Ahh, but there is, my boy.''

''The Regnum is the only thing that keeps people from each other's throats!'' Radis was angry now. Bolla was attacking his deepest convictions, and he was frustrated by his failure to get closer to the assassin. In contrast, Bolla's eyes were twinkling.

''That may be, my boy. But what is it that *puts* people at each other's throats. *That* is the important question. The answer—if there is an answer—can only be found in history and what it can teach us about ourselves.''

He stalled Radis only a second. ''*That* may be, Doctor. But while the old men are ruminating, while they're rummaging leisurely through the ragbag of history, civilization in the present tense will be crumbling to pieces around their doddering ankles!''

Bolla was unperturbed. ''The young always say that.''

''It's always true!''

''Then perhaps we should let it crumble.'' Bolla brought his shoulders up the few centimeters necessary to make his neck disappear. ''That will become history too. It may provide the great lesson that we need.''

''The lesson has already been learned.'' Tyrees spoke softly, as if to himself, as if from a sleep that had brought dreams of lonely revelation and sad hope. Radis and Bolla had forgotten him, something they were both startled to discover was possible —but Bolla was the first to hear beyond the sounds of the words to their meaning. He leaned forward, dubious but willing to believe, like one of his own hungry students from a time long past.

"When, Pol?"

"The Tercians. They learned." Tyrees lifted his head and stared at them, embers of defiance firing his eyes. It was then that Bolla realized fully why those eyes always disturbed him. It was because he felt them sensually, as he would feel the heat from the sun as a breach in the clouds passed under it.

Tyrees rose to his feet and moved to the balcony window and the night sky that filled it. Like a moth to fire, the speckled blackness seemed to draw him.

"Tercet was cut off from the galaxy by the black hole for a thousand years," he said. "For a thousand years she had no wars, no struggles for power. Nothing in *galactic* history matches that."

"I know that, but *why?* Was it the New Covenant?" Bolla had to speak across the room to the face in the glass, as he had weeks earlier when the killer of minds was only a shadow. He had a sense of déjà vu. "Was it the New Covenant, Pol?"

"No, the Learning was a product, not a cause. It was because they had to help each other to survive. They fought, all right, but they had to fight *together*—or they would die. The black hole was there to remind them. It almost took them once, so they knew what it was to look death in the face and be spared."

As he spoke, they could see the back of his clean skull, but his voice came from a far place, from the shimmer of his face in the window surrounded by darkness. "The first colonists looked at it for days—weeks—expecting to be drawn with their ship into the hole. Then a decimal point, followed by many zeros, followed by a one digit number, saved them all. This absurd quantity, hardly more than nothing itself, was the measure of their escape velocity. *Forger's* captain called it 'an angel's breath' because it was enough to prevent them from going into a tight spiral orbit around the black hole. Instead, their course was bent like a kink in a rope, and they were slung into Tercet's tri-star system.''

Tyrees turned back to them. Bolla blinked, for he had expected the face in the dark glass to speak. "You know that they had to abandon *Forger*. Her navigation system had been inoperative since long before the black hole. Afterward, she went out into intergalactic space. . . . I've often wanted to chase and find her. I probably can, you know. She's over a thousand years old now, and . . ."

Tyrees's words died off, faded into silence, like *Forger* herself. Radis put him back on course.

"Then they had to deal with Tercet. That's part of it, isn't it?"

"Yes. The experts would term her 'dubious marginal'— meaning that she probably couldn't sustain life without terra-forming or extensive off-planet support. The shipwrecked colonists had neither, but they survived. They thought she was Nirvana, simply because she was a chance for life, and that was more than they dared ask for. To them she was a miracle. Life was a miracle. Through the course of a thousand years Tercet bred the Seers. She bred Meta-sol . . . she bred me." Tyrees stopped and frowned as if he had suddenly remembered his audience. "Yes," he added bitterly, "the Tercians learned their lesson."

Bolla had been on Tercet for a bare three days—time enough only for the Seers to be summoned for their departure after he had brought Tyrees the warning about the Chairman's intentions. Tyrees, Pol-Nesol-Rast, had been among them only seven months; yet they came to him and accepted the loss of their home like children following a father. They were technological-ly primitive, but every one of the Seers possessed abilities Bolla could never hope to understand, let alone emulate.

It was a time of crisis and haste, so he took away from Tercet only two strong memories: hot, blowing red sand that blasted the skin, and the black hole in the night sky. It was indeed a black hole, defined by a straggle-edged ring of stars, and it was impossible to keep his eyes away from it for long.

Radis had joined Tyrees at the window. "I want to come with you, Vitar."

"Oh? Where?"

"To Tercet. I've never been there."

Tyrees smiled thinly. "Not many have. Technically, it's debatable that Tercet is even part of the galaxy. A difficult run for the best of ships out there where the galactic pathways are thin, especially with the Hole to circumnavigate. That's why she was isolated for so long."

"I know you're going there, Vitar. I want to come with you."

"Don't be so keen, Radis," piped up Bolla from his chair. "Trips with the Vitar tend to be stressful. I can vouch."

Tyrees looked back at him, but there was no humor in his expression. "A few minutes ago you were hinting about strong measures, Radis. Let's hear them." He strode back to the grouping of chairs and sat, forcing Radis to follow.

"Very well." Radis sat also, and pointed at the table, its surface now opaqued. "My work-up is all in there. It *is* drastic, but I see no realistic alternative—unless we want to continue chasing the killer's tracks around the galaxy just to pick up the corpses of the men who now keep the New Covenant a-live."

"Huh!" grunted Bolla. "I'm already apprehensive."

"So am I, Doctor, but the longer we delay decisive action, the more variables came into play. Public reaction is just one of them. The old guard won't hesitate to take advantage of something like this—consider Singletary an object lesson."

"Touché. I'm listening." Bolla settled back, fingers laced across his paunch. "But I hope the cure isn't worse than the disease."

"It's just an extension of the Vitar's original plan to trap our man on Singletary, really, although it's a massive operation. First, we prohibit *all* interstellar travel." Bolla emitted a low whistle, but Radis ignored it. "And we enforce it rigorously. At the very least this will bring him to ground, even if he has control of a vessel. Next, we do a comprehensive computer search of all those making landfall on the victim's planets at the appropriate times. I know that this probably won't turn up even a physical identity, but it will narrow the search down. We've already been able to eliminate all the legitimate Seers as possible suspects."

Bolla's fingers remained laced, but now they were forming a platform for his bowed forehead. He spoke to Radis with his fuzzy pate foremost. "Radis, the Regnum *exists* because of trade. An edict forbidding interstellar travel will create an absolute furor. We couldn't make it stick."

"We can make it stick for a while," said Radis. "We simply have to try—unless you want to sit back and continue the body count."

Bolla raised his head slowly. "As I said, your cure will kill the patient." His eyes shone dully with a glaze of fatigue born of something more than lack of rest, of something that spoke of burdens carried too long and too far. Radis recognized the look and turned away, reluctant to push his case in spite of his conviction. Both, by unspoken agreement, waited.

Tyrees took his time. As usual he was as still as stone. As of stone were the sharp, fine planes of his face. But the eyes, always the eyes, betrayed the stone. They flickered, twisting to the cuts of some whip-wielding devil within. Radis could read them better because of the acuteness of senses sharpened by the Learning, but Bolla knew more of the devil. Nevertheless, they were both surprised when he smiled.

"I've noticed this phenomenon often," he said. "You are both right, and you contradict each other. It can be disconcerting."

"We have to act," said Radis.

"Radis, how can you accompany me to Tercet—to chase a wild goose—if you have to oversee such a massive operation?"

Radis answered decisively. "You think he'll be there. I know you do. And I have competent people to run things here."

Tyrees rose. He walked to the dim hallway and turned at its

entrance. "No. I need you here, especially now. Issue the edict, but limit it to worlds that have Seers. Announce that it's a temporary measure, and give them a week's warning before it's put into effect. That should reduce the hue and cry, and if the killer is Meta-sol's mysterious Uni-shad, he may take to ground on Tercet. I leave in six hours."

"But Vitar . . ." Radis was speaking to his back. Tyrees's voice came back to him hollowly from the recesses of the corridor.

"Do it, please."

She was precisely the same, down to the rhythm of her slow, shallow breathing. It was difficult even for him to detect the rise and fall of her breast under the coverlet, but it was there, and it was the same. Its ebb and flow mesmerized him. The mask, too, clung to its hard perfection. Time seemed the victim here, not Shaamlik.

When he finally moved, it was to lift and pull back the coverlet, slowly, down the length of her body. The figure revealed on the bed reminded him of the lifelike, milky stone of Monoman's statues, but it was not seductive. It was merely beautiful, more dead than the stone, more fragile than the mask. It erased the illusion of permanence. Soft nubs of bone pushed up from beneath skin that had once sheathed firm muscle; there was space between her thighs where flesh had receded; her breasts had flattened against the cages of her ribs. But she was still beautiful. The mask did not diminish that. She was simply some alien form of beauty, a macabre goddess worshiped with unknowable fervor and strange rites. Only the coiled snake of translucent tubing marred that beauty.

A shudder passed through his body. A high squeak of sound, like that of a frightened rodent, was wrung from him, violating, tearing ragged edges into the silence of the room. It was cut off abruptly. He reached for the tubing with trembling fingers and pinched it closed.

He waited for a time. The figure on the bed remained as it was, the mask still perfect. Then, not trusting his tremulous fingers, he pulled the tubing to his mouth and clenched it between his teeth. The giver of life waited.

Slowly the rhythm of breathing decayed into gentle spasms, small, soundless heaves at her throat. The clean, expressionless mask moved to one side, then the other.

He spat out the tubing and fled.

Twelve

I find it fascinating to come under the influence of such a . . . a negativity. I know of its influence because I see nothing there. Like trying to look down inside yourself, something I intend to do more. Watery stars at its periphery, becoming fewer as we approach.

—From the captain's log of Forger

CONDOR SLID SMOOTHLY off the pathway, and every eye was on the bridge screen. Only Tyrees knew what it would look like, having seen it once before; nevertheless, his attention was the most rapt.

The screen fought off its electronic fuzz as the optics computer eliminated the garbage and began to build its simulation from the sensor data. Like diamond dust smeared upon black velvet, dim stars gained resolution near the edges of the screen. That was all. The bridge crew waited for more, expectantly, until they realized they were looking at it. They felt cheated for a moment, but the feeble glimmers of light around it were a testimony to its power. The phenomenon could have no other name. A black hole.

Tyrees always thought of it as an invisible octopus sitting silent and dark and deadly in the nether depths of the cosmic sea. On that scale it was a very small one, but it was the closest to the galaxy by hundreds of light-years, and it was still the most powerful natural force with which man had come into contact—if contact can be applied to his awed and careful circling of it, like a pilgrim around a distant volcano. The rare visitors to Tercet were compelled to come as *Condor* had, along a galactic pathway that trailed its fading tendril several light-years beyond the last thin spiral of stars into the Greater Void. Only the most skilled navigators with the best of equipment would attempt the journey, and this was only its first leg. Gaining the as yet invisible tri-star of Tercet also required a circumnavigation of the hole under conventional power. The crew was well aware that this was unnecessary for Tyrees, given his ability to use the intergalactic pathways, but they never questioned his orders and were grateful for the chance to "see" the black hole.

Those on the bridge stared without speaking at the rough circle of blackness for a long time, each thinking thoughts of his own, each finding in the hole an inexplicable link with another thing of potency and darkness inside them. But such thoughts cannot be sustained. One by one a strange, restless anxiety pulled the eyes of the bridge crew from the screen and they turned their attention to their instruments.

Except Tyrees. As Condor approached the hole, as the delicate swath of stars at the edges of the hole grew thinner, the angry blue of his eyes grew deeper. He sat in the command chair glaring at the hole as if his being were the sole object of its terrible drawing power. The captain was standing beside him, and he found the black hole easier to look upon than those deadly blue eyes. When the last of the stars were threatening to bleed off the edges of the screen, he finally prodded with his voice.

"Sir? . . . Sir?"

Tyrees didn't move, but after a time he responded. "Yes."

"We're getting too close, sir. Much closer than this, and even light is drawn in."

"*Forger* went closer than this, Captain, and she was a very primitive machine."

"Yes sir, but this thing is unpredictable. We don't know

enough. Instruments are unreliable.''

His words were instantly prophetic. SCANCOM had turned toward them. ''Readings have gone crazy, sir! I have a distance reading twice what it was a moment ago. It seems to be reversing!''

''Cut power to zero,'' said Tyrees. ''We'll float in for a while.''

''Yes, sir,'' said NAVCOM. ''Zero power.''

The captain was suddenly very frightened, but he managed to keep his voice under control. ''But sir, who knows what effects that thing can have? The engines . . . we might not be *able* to regain power.''

Tyrees shrugged, but said nothing. For the first time in many years of service dedicated to this man, the captain felt an anger upwell.

At close to the speed of light, a speed Tyrees had referred to as ''floating,'' *Condor* was sucked down into the gravity well of the hole. Soon the last of the stars fled the edges of the screen until it was a dark slate. The captain looked back and forth between it and Tyrees. The hand he had rested on the back of the command chair gradually turned into a claw.

''Sir. We can go no farther.''

Tyrees's naked head stirred only slightly. ''The New Covenant was born here, Captain.''

''Sir?''

''Almost *exactly* here. In the mind of *Forger*'s captain. His log is the precursor to *The Teraac*.''

The captain squirmed. He could see the lines of fear etching subtly into the muscles on the backs of his bridge crew. Tyrees finally turned in the command chair to face him.

''Let them feel it, Captain. Let us *all* feel it. *He* did—*for weeks*—as *Forger* was being drawn into the hole. So did several hundred colonists, the first Tercians. They had no instrumentation, and no hope. They didn't *think* they were going to die, they *knew* it, knew it for all that time, even though it turned out that they were wrong as far as the hole was concerned. Still, they weren't *really* wrong, were they?''

Is he testing our courage? thought the captain. Is this—this man-god suffering some kind of megalomania? His response was sound only, the sound of his words a pitiful shield held up ridiculously to cover his fear.

"I . . . I don't see how . . . I don't see why we are . . ."

"It was the beginning of it all—what happened to him here. He set the Tercians on the path. There are phrases . . . metaphors, even ideas . . ." Tyrees's voice trailed off.

The captain looked at the black screen, sucked in between his teeth a soft piece of his inner cheek and clamped down on it. When he found the pain insufficient, he clamped harder, until he felt the gristle split and tasted blood. Then he was able to glance around the bridge and note a particularly steel-backed technic.

"RECOM."

"Uh, yessir!"

"Relax, RECOM. You are being treated to a very special tourist's delight. Enjoy it."

"Yessir."

Tyrees smiled. "His words in the log. They're echoed in *The Teraac*—and the Seers' way of speaking too. Especially Metasol. The Captain of *Forger* saw something here."

With his new, hard-won calm, the captain was able to think. "Perhaps he saw what was *always* true," he said. "Perhaps he saw that we were born to die."

Tyrees looked at him sharply. "That was the last time I will ever underestimate you, Captain." He turned back to the blank screen. "Perhaps, also, he saw that we were made to fight it. And that everything else was a false enemy? A substitute for harder battles? Is that it, Captain?"

The captain also looked at the screen, and suddenly the pain in his mouth was not enough. "I don't know, sir," he said.

"Neither do I."

Tyrees looked once again at the screen and closed his eyes. "NAVCOM."

"Yes, sir."

"Get us out of here."

Eyes still closed, he continued speaking softly as the bridge crew performed the rituals of technology, the rites of numbers and machines that had been created to ward off the darkness as *Condor* moved through the epitome of alien territory.

"Absurd notion—fighting death. Ridiculous. Meta-sol says we must accept. . . . The Maker wills it, I suppose. . . . some Maker . . . I have about the same chance against Uni-shad."

The captain did not understand, but he said nothing.

Thirteen

Screened from the galaxy by the black hole is a most magnificent, most unusual star system. Three stars—a red giant, a blue dwarf, and a yellow class G—dance in a complex synchronous orbit that is utterly spectacular. . . . We accept this miracle. Imagine! With its size alone, the cosmos only fails to humble the ignorant. Yet it provided us—less significant in the scale of things than an amoeba to a star—with a chance for life.

—From the captain's log of Forger

CONDOR'S METALLIC SKIN was a moving rainbow. Her speed and angle of entry were such that the three lights of the tri-star vied with one another, played in ripples along one side of *Condor* as she stooped toward Tercet. Tyrees was alone in the observation chamber, standing close to the glasteel bubble. To him, the bridge screen had always been a barrier, a curtain before his eyes; so was the bubble, but it was better. He stared with pleasure at the three balls of light, knowing they would take on colors when they fell through Tercet's atmosphere. He was certain he felt something akin to what the captain of *Forger* felt. Yes, he thought. It had its beginnings here—and so did I. The black hole and the tri-star, both painted forever in their sky, never let them forget; both were stamped on every page of *The Teraac*. He remembered a passage he had read into the field report that had eventually made him a traitor.

Behold Eros: vast and consuming, a blood-gorged passion.
Behold Sentos: delicate and moving, an azure caress.

Behold Logos: piercing and bright, a searing gold. With these lights ye can fuel, feel, see. Then behold the single light, the trilight. Use it to *know*.

First, ye must be asked: does Sentos rule Logos, or Logos Eros? Can ye then allow the slicing blade of reason to let flow passion's blood, or the heat of passion to devour the gentle senses?

Each is a gift of knowing, but each alone reveals only a pale shadow of truth. To see by one light only is to be drawn into the Hole of Darkness from which there is no returning.

The passage had played like a whimsical ghost in the attic of his mind for many years, and each year brought another nuance to its meaning. He wondered if his modifications were truly a function of a growing understanding, or simply changes in his own outlook. Pure scientists—or cynics—would see *The Teraac* as they saw all mystical writing; it said to the believer what he wanted it to say.

Condor approached its orbital path. Tercet was small, reddish, innocuous. The absence of blue, the rarity of cloud, told of its history. Water was scarce. Life was a grudging reward for Sisyphean struggle; adding to the *quality* of that life was an outrageous defiance. So it was that their scant thousands had scrabbled at the brutal soil for centuries so that a few Seers had the time to scrabble at the soil of their minds. Their Seers were their living saints, their legacy, a wondrous gift to the lost galaxy beyond the black hole—and now, one by one, the Seers were dying.

Tyrees looked down on the bleak, precious planet and wondered how it could have bred both the Seers and a potent agent of their destruction. A deadly microbe had incubated within the healing vaccine? A killer virus had been spawned from blood and hope? Perhaps it had not, perhaps evil could not be a seedling of goodness. But he must find out. If the New Covenant were only the stuff of dreams and wishes, if *The*

Teraac were only a child's fascination with the impossible, he must find that out too. He realized that even if both answers were in the negative, he would still have an enemy whose powers seemed invincible; but he could take heart, he could have cause.

A speaker sounded. "Captain here, sir. We are about to enter our orbit. A shuttle will be ready in a few minutes."

Tyrees stepped on the red Tercian earth as he had for the first time six years earlier, as a Cadre One. As it had then, the ubiquitous wind took his cape and swirled it around his legs, once again declaring its superfluity here. He looked up (on Tercet the eyes are always drawn skyward) at her three suns: Eros, the fierce red giant; Logos, the yellow-gold ball of most man-supporting worlds; Sentos, the small, faded blue dwarf. The last was at this time gradually disappearing into the others' glare. Calculating their movements in conjunction with each other and Tercet herself was a mathematician's nightmare; but the unpredictable, shifting colors drifting across the canvas of the sky, especially when the suns were all close to the horizon, was a painter's dream.

Tyrees brought his eyes down to watch the Emissary and an assistant coming toward him, holding their official robes close against the hot wind. He greeted them with the Cadre salute.

"Officer Ttig Hal, Cadre One. Nice of you to meet me, sir."

"Our pleasure, Officer Hal." The middle-aged professional offered a genial hand. "We get few visitors, as you know, so even the Cadre is welcome." He smiled broadly to emphasize the humor. Emissary staffs were the diplomatic arms of the Regnum, and one was present on every member planet. Relations with the Cadre had not always been cordial.

"I gather things are usually quiet here," said Tyrees.

"They are indeed. Aside from some freighter traffic, there's not much to keep us busy, I'm afraid. Tercet is called the Vitar's birthplace—only a metaphorical truth, of course—but the risky passage still keeps most outsiders away." Gesturing, he began to walk Tyrees toward a cluster of small stone buildings in the distance. "We have been getting some specialists lately, though."

"Specialists?"

"Yes. Medical types—psychologists mostly—anthropologists, even a philosopher or two. Trying to tap the source, I suppose." The Emissary was warming to a favorite topic, and his hands became animated. "Just *what* gave birth to the New Covenant? It *is* a fascinating question, is it not? I've begun to dip into it myself."

Tyrees read his voice and gestures. In spite of the man's diplomatic metier, he was an easy study. The Emissary was both embarrassed and enthusiastic, like a man taken with a boy's hobby.

"Really? Are you receiving training?"

The Emissary glanced back at his assistant, who was digging sand out of his eyes a few paces behind them. He lowered his voice. "Well, I am, actually. From Kreat-mel."

"Tercet's Seer. The one sent back after the coup?"

"That's right. An amazing man. I don't know how he finds the time for an old dabbler like me."

"Why not? You're an important man—you're Tercet's contact with the galaxy." This touch of flattery was just for the making of conversation as they walked along, but the Emissary's response caused Tyrees to consider something forgotten.

"When the Seers fled, they left behind the best of a whole generation in their trainees, you know. They had been abandoned to their own devices for several years, so they were ecstatic when Kreat-mel returned."

Was it possible? Could one of the unmentored trainees—some of them surely close to the level of Seer—have mutated himself into the killer? The Emissary prattled on, and Tyrees considered the question dubiously until he felt the air, *heard* the air crackle. It was like the tremor of a skin of winter ice underfoot. He stopped and looked to a horizon of low hills. There, tiny and alone in the distance, the off-white of his shawl barely distinguishable against the ochre of his surroundings, stood the unmistakable figure of a Seer. Tyrees could just make out the cane as it was raised, perhaps in greeting.

The Emissary followed Tyrees's eyes to the spot in the hills and squinted.

"What is it? See something?" The figure turned and moved without haste until it disappeared behind a knoll.

"No, nothing, I guess."

The Emissary chuckled. "I know what you mean. Happens to me all the time here. It's the light, I suppose, and the color shifts. Tercet isn't a good place if you're given to hallucinations, Officer Hal."

They resumed their pace. In the heat the Emissary's brow began to glisten in spite of the dryness of the air. Tyrees could hear his breathing thicken as they started up the slope that led to the fringes of the village.

"Whew! Not getting any younger. . . . I wish they would permit *some* kind of transportation on this ball of sand. Not even beasts of burden here, you know—except the Tercians themselves." He looked keenly at Tyrees. "I hope you won't have to be moving around a lot. This is a rough climate for travelers not used to it."

Tyrees knew that the man was fishing. The Emissary had been informed only of the arrival of a Cadre One. The only other Number One who had ever set foot on Tercet bore a name that was fading from common memory—Pol Tyrees. The Emissary had to guess that something very important must be happening. Tyrees was about to ignore the bait when another picture of the man's face, a younger face, surfaced in his mind. Silently, he cursed himself. Was he so preoccupied now that his memory was faulty?

"You have been Tercet's Emissary since Tercet was rediscovered, haven't you? You're Neet Pristor?"

"Yes, I've been here nine years. . . . By the way, please call me Neet. Everyone else insists upon calling me by my title except my wife, and she died two years ago."

Pristor spoke with simple sincerity, and it dawned on Tyrees that he was a lonely man, perhaps for reasons in addition to his lonely posting. History, too, inclined Tyrees to trust him.

"You were the Tercians' prisoner at one point, weren't you?"

Pristor's face was a bland, featureless moon, until he smiled. Then it filled like a balloon into the form it was meant to take. It was the face of a man who always looked for humor and had found too little of it.

"Yes, and a damn good thing too. They warned me that the Chairman was sending one of his little toys to dump the whole planet into oblivion. I *believed* them when our scanner picked up the sign of one of those bloody juggernauts—class XL's—on its way. The Tercians allowed me to send a message to it. I told them I knew their purpose and that the Seers had escaped."

Pristor stopped just as they stepped onto the main street of the village of Luta. It was packed hard, even rutted in places, by the pressure of a thousand years of walking feet. The entrances to some of the hutlike structures boasted the luxury of stone walkways. The smile was still on Pristor's face, but his head was tilted curiously as he looked at Tyrees and his raised hand halted his assistant a few paces behind them, out of earshot.

"The commander of that battlefleet vessel was going to go through with his chore anyway, but a Cadre man stopped him. He saved a whole planet's worth of lives, including mine. He was a Number One, like you . . . he even had the same *name* as you. . . . I had the privilege of shaking his hand."

Tyrees nodded and returned the smile. "So you were left here by the Chairman to fester quietly in isolation, stuck behind a black hole, with no way of spreading nasty stories."

"Yep. But I have no regrets. I like it here now."

"And then, after the coup, you were forgotten."

"I suppose so. . . . On the other hand, Tercian is a very difficult language, you know, and Tercet is a very special place. It needs someone who knows it. Perhaps they thought it best to leave me here."

"If that was their thinking, they were wise." Tyrees thought of Bolla, and knew that to be the case. Pristor's smile broadened.

"Are you going to tell me who you are—and why you're here?"

"I'm going to need your help."

The two men continued their walk down the earthen street, which was taking on a violet hue as the two larger suns were setting. Aside from the man trailing behind them, no one else was to be seen, for Tercet was a place where almost everyone worked in the distant fields to stay alive. Everyone but the Seers.

Fourteen

When the time of choice comes, only the very wise know that it has also come before.

— *The Sayings of Meta-sol*

"AND YOU ARE the Vitar?"

"Yes."

Light from the fire licked at dark corners. The Emissary's private quarters were a cosy clutter of contradictions. Tercet's rough practicality flickered with the firelight off the studded stone of the walls and the uneven, footworn patina of the ceramic floor; a galactic technocracy obtruded here and there in the form of a recording machine and crystals, an intercom that was connected to the working office of the small staff, and a modest terminal. The third element was the most pervasive; it was made up of the paraphernalia of a curious and eclectic mind, and the softer, more aesthetic touches of a woman. A piece of crudely carved bone—possibly human—nestled comfortably beneath an arrangement of delicate artificial flowers. An ancient book rested on the mantle over the fireplace, beside the muted but exotic glory of a fabric hanging from some place many light-years away.

Pristor was in a state of shock. In the unsteady light the furrows of age on his face deepened. He sat limply in his deep chair nearest the fire and stared at Tyrees.

"Have my eyes or my memory become that bad? Why did I not recognize you?"

"I have changed somewhat," said Tyrees with a rueful smile. "And this hair—and the eye color—are not mine."

Pristor's voice dropped to a near whisper. "You are a *god* here, did you know that? No, not *a* god, *the* god."

Tyrees's false eyebrows lifted. "Am I a god to you?"

"I . . . no, I suppose not. But there are so many things . . . I don't know what you are."

"I am a man."

"Not an ordinary man."

"Nor are you."

Pristor laughed, and the lines of his face reformed, his tension and his years leavened. "Yes, of course. I am an *extraordinary* man—an old and minor diplomat tucked away behind a black hole, struggling with new notions of life that tantalize but mystify him. Would you trade places with me?" Pristor's quite genuine laughter faded to a chuckle, but it was cut short.

"Yes."

Pristor's voice took on a cutting edge. "You flatter me, sir. Unnecessarily. I will, of course, do what I can to help you, though I can't imagine what that might be."

Tyrees looked around the room, his eyes coming to rest upon the flowers before returning to Pristor. "You are not an ordinary man but not because you have lost someone you considered an essential part of you." Pristor's face went white. Tyrees continued in a manner that was almost clinical. "That happens to many. You are unique because you do more than just go on living. You *wish* to go on living—and you bring her *with* you. Yes, I wish I could trade places with you."

Pristor looked at him like a child whose father had just wiped away his tears. After a time he pulled himself to his feet to stand before the fire. His hands clasped and unclasped behind his back as he stared into it.

"I am beginning to understand what a Seer can see," he said. "Thank you for the compliment." He prodded at the fire for a moment with a foot before returning to his chair. "So we have a killer—a very potent killer—who you believe sprouted out of Tercet's infertile soil. His name may or may not be Uni-shad. What can I do to help?"

"If he's here, and I don't know that he is, he may well get to me before I get to him. . . ." Tyrees hesitated, fingering the shimmering black cloth of his cape.

"Yes? Go ahead. You've really only to order me, after all."

"There are some things no one should—no one *can* be ordered to do."

Tyrees looked at him long and hard, and Pristor knew that he would not like what he was about to hear. "Go ahead, Vitar."

"You must understand that if this man takes me, he can take *anyone.* He could not be stopped, unless destroyed—or at least isolated. If in a month you do not speak again to me personally, you must message the Cadre Proctor under my code to place Tercet under quarantine—*permanent* quarantine—if you consider one hundred years to be permanent."

Pristor nodded as if he had just taken an order to arrange a banquet. He rose from his chair again, and with the deliberation of a man under sedation, knelt to place what looked like gnarled roots on the fire. It hissed and flamed higher, throwing heat and light that seemed out of proportion to its fuel.

"No physical contact for a hundred years," he said in a musing voice as light and shadow played on his face.

"None. Unless you want a murderer as Vitar."

"There is no . . . less extreme measure?"

Tyrees's words were as dark and soft as the cape that enfolded him. "It is the *least* extreme measure. The sure way would be to obliterate the planet."

"I need a drink." Still moving like an automaton, Pristor opened a small cabinet near the fireplace and removed a decanter and glasses. Tyrees shook his head when one glass was

proffered in his direction. Very carefully, Pristor poured a
measure for himself. Very carefully, he sipped.

"This is my first brandy since I began my . . . what are they?
Lessons? Lessons with Kreat-mel. I'm ultimately supposed to
control my own body chemistry, I guess. But I've always known
I wouldn't live long enough to get that far." Standing in the
middle of the room, he looked up, seemingly to watch the play
of firelight between the heavy beams of the ceiling.

"Will you do it?" Tyrees asked the question without
inflection. Pristor answered with a question of his own, his eyes
still lifted to the ceiling.

"What do you think will happen *here*—if Tercet is cut off?"

"He would rule here. He would have to take what he could
get. You—and the others—would be his playthings. That's
what he has done so far. Play."

"He would be angry, wouldn't he? I mean . . . he hasn't
exactly been *playing*, has he? He's been methodical, purpos-
ive."

"His purpose would be thwarted."

In a swift motion Pristor downed his brandy and looked at the
empty glass. "One hundred years. Ironic . . . for a *thousand*
years Tercet was alone. Like an exiled son. You've probably
heard them say it—'our fathers of the hidden stars.' Now they
might be asked to do it again, only this time they'll have more
than their environment to fight."

"Will you do it?"

Pristor looked at the spray of impossibly delicate flowers.
"Of course I will do it. . . . I can *say* that—I can even *believe*
it—but can I really *do* it? Who knows. I will try."

Tyrees nodded, but said nothing. Pristor returned to the
cabinet to refill his glass. He was too restless to sit. After
toasting the play of light on the ceiling again, he stood in the
center of the room with his head cocked to one side, perhaps
listening to the crackle of the fire. Every so often he flicked a
glance at the dark figure slumped in the chair farthest from the
fire. When it flared he saw the hard, clearly defined features of a
bone-white face so impregnably impassive that it seemed the

product of some natural sculpting, like the chance artifice of a swift river on ancient rock. He began to move around at random, touching, peering closely, nodding and muttering, in his own room a tourist in a museum of quaint artifacts.

He came to a halt at a set of silken drapes, their sensual luxury also declaring a non-Tercian source and the gentle spell of a feminine taste. More than anything else in the room, they softened the effect of the implacably hard and heavy stone. He drew them aside to reveal a window. It was made of thick, pebbled glass, impregnated with impurities, and it represented the height of Tercian technology. Looking through such a medium, one could never be certain of the accuracy of what one saw. Its texture imposed subtle distortions on outside objects, but what was distortion and what reality was difficult to discern.

The tri-star had set, but there were still shadows of light whispering color into the night air. The wind moaned softly. Not far above the horizon, a blurred line that separated shades of darkness, hung the black hole. A shaggy, round rim of stars, a ring of desperate glowing made of the most precious jewelry of the cosmos, struggled to keep contained—nothing. The spectacle dominated Tercet's night sky with its motionless drama.

When Pristor finally turned from the window, he found that his guest's eyes were on it too. As the firelight faded, its colors dying gently on the stone walls, the man in black blinked once and returned his look. Pristor felt a moment of impossible communion with this strange man who preferred darkness to fire, yet ruled a galaxy.

"You know, even after all these years I can't get used to that," he said.

"The black hole? No. It's not something you get used to."

Pristor thought about this, not sure if he meant anything in particular or was just responding out of courtesy. He gave it up and reached for a small bronzed bell. "There's someone you should meet," he said, sounding it.

In a moment a man appeared in the doorway. He was short

and set solidly, like the walls of the house itself, but there was not a gram of excess fat on him. This, as much as the belted homespun of his shirt and trousers, proclaimed him a Tercian. He stood silently until Pristor turned from the window.

"Oh, there you are, Clad. Where are your mates?"

"In the kitchen, Emissary." His voice was quiet—respectful, but in no way obsequious.

"Bring them in, will you? I want you all to meet this gentleman." After a glance at Tyrees, the man left. Pristor smiled. "You know of their triad custom?" Tyrees nodded. "I wanted to hire only one, but of course I ended up with three. They don't make very good servants, I'm afraid. Too independent."

"Not independent," said Tyrees. "They've had to cooperate for survival here. They simply have no concept of servitude because everyone's job is considered essential. Tercet has no hierarchy in any social sense, except for the Seers—and *their* function is not social."

"Of course, you're right. I keep forgetting that you know these people." Pristor added another clutch of roots to the fire. It hissed brightly again and a light wave of incense reminded them pleasantly of the ineffable odor that had always been there. "And I'm not complaining. Clad's triad is a great help to the staff. They only get grouchy when they're idle—or when they see *us* being idle."

Clad returned with two others, a woman and another man. The woman was a string bean, sinewy and tall. The man was even shorter than Clad, but small boned and pixyish. They were as unlike as could be, except for the blandness of their expressions; indeed, their natural air of secure and competent grimness saved them from appearing comic. Tyrees rose from his chair as Pristor made the introductions.

"Clad, Mart, Letr, this is Officer Hal. He has important work to do here. I would like you to consent to help him in any way you can."

Letr, the woman, took a step forward. She was automatically assuming one of her triad functions as its spokesperson on formal occasions. She looked at Tyrees closely, taking in the long cape with special attention.

"You wear a thing like the Vitar did—before he became a Seer. I saw him ourself when he first came here."

"That's right," said Pristor. "The Vitar worked then with the same organization—the Cadre. It keeps the laws among the planets."

"We know that," sniffed Letr, reluctantly impressed. "Why are you here? Tercet breaks no laws."

"He is looking for a man—a Seer."

Letr shrugged. "Kreat-mel. He needs no help for that. Tercet is left with only one Seer. Clad saw him ourself not long ago. Why do you need our help?"

"Perhaps . . ." said Pristor hesitantly, "this man *used* to be a Seer. His name is Uni-shad."

"A Seer is always a Seer," snorted Letr. "We know of no one of that name."

"Tell me something, Letr," said Tyrees, speaking for the first time. "Are you—the Tercians—angry because you have lost your Seers to the Regnum?"

Letr flicked a glance at her two men. Tyrees noted the small action as indicative. It was very difficult for a Tercian to construct a deliberate lie spontaneously. For their spokesperson to say something that the others of the triad might disagree with was a gaff of considerable proportions, and they spoke as individuals only about things considered unimportant; so their normal alternatives were silence, or the bald truth.

"Yes, we feel . . . resentment at the loss of our Seers. Kreat-mel cannot guide us well alone. Few words have been added to *The Teraac*."

Tyrees nodded, a frown creasing his forehead. A Seer had three functions: to struggle along the path of self-knowledge, to record his progress in *The Teraac*, and to guide his people. "You must know," he said, "that Tercet is now called the Seed World. To us of the hidden stars, this is a holy place. The Seers must minister to a whole galaxy, Letr, and pass on their knowledge. It is a great burden for them and for you, but already there are new Seers who have never seen the tri-star.''

Letr looked at her men again and, as if at a signal, their eyes fell in shame. "Yes, so Kreat-mel has told us. We are . . . honored, and proud." Then she lifted her head, having paid their due, and gave in to human petulance. "But we still miss our Seers. In the mornings when we walked to the fields to tend the grain and bring it water, every village met its Seer along the way to touch his cane."

Tyrees felt a pang in his heart. Suddenly Tercet seemed so fragile, an exquisite piece of china serving a delicacy offered to feasting barbarians. He turned and walked to the window where the ring of stars lit the black sky. He spoke self-consciously, but it was in the language of *The Teraac*.

"In time," he said, "Tercet will bring forth new Seers. She is already known as the spawning ground of man's salvation. In time, she will bring the light of the tri-star to us all."

Letr stared at his back. "Are you a Seer from the hidden stars?" Tyrees's spine stiffened. She hurled her words at him. "Where is your cane?"

He turned to face her. "No. Not yet. But I was once Meta-sol's student. Soon, perhaps."

Letr smiled for the first time. Her elongated face, an ugly face that spoke of duty always given but rarely acknowledged, became a thing of beauty. "You are a child of Meta-sol! He was *our* Seer—Luta's Seer, the greatest of them all. The father of the Vitar!"

"Yes . . . I know."

"Can you tell us when he will come?"

Pristor frowned. "Surely you know that Meta-sol is dead, Letr."

Letr responded triumphantly. "No, he is not. He lives in the Vitar, and the Vitar will return to us. So it is written!"

Pristor stretched his neck, tilting back his head and pointing his jaw as if in fatigue. He cleared his throat noisily.

"Then it will come to be," said Tyrees quietly, "but who am I to say when?" Abruptly he moved from the window into the shadows farthest from the fire. He pulled his cape more closely around himself. "Tell me, Letr. Have you heard of anything . . . *strange* over the past years since the Seers left? An unexplained death, perhaps? Someone with unusual powers?"

Letr glanced again at her two men before shaking her head. "We have heard nothing like that. You must see Kreat-mel."

"I will," said Tyrees. "Thank you for your help." He bowed slightly in the accepted Tercian fashion. All three returned the bow and filed from the room. Tyrees could hear their hushed whispers begin as soon as they thought themselves out of earshot.

"One of Meta-sol's children!"

"Yes! What can he be looking for?"

"Strange questions . . . strange man!"

The whispers faded down the hall as Pristor returned to his chair. "Pardon me for sitting, Vitar," he said, grinning impishly, "but I've had too much to drink—and just being present when prophesy is fulfilled always makes me a bit shaky."

Tyrees smiled thinly. "Kreat-mel must have added to *The Teraac*," he mused. "That is only done when a Seer has something new, something certain to say."

Pristor's grin disappeared instantly. "Hummph . . . well. Do you think Kreat-mel knows something? Something he knew would bring you here eventually?"

"I don't know. But Kreat-mel is one of the old guard. He's been a Seer for thirty years or more. It may also be that Meta-sol had a reason to select *him* and not another to return here."

"And that reason may have something to do with Uni-shad?"

Tyrees sighed deeply. Pristor could actually watch his face sagging within seconds, losing its customary tone, fall into the slack of fatigue, the gravity of burden.

"It's all conjecture," he said. "I'd better rest now. I'll see Kreat-mel tomorrow. There may be some answers then."

"Tomorrow? I don't know if he's anywhere *near* Luta. I haven't seen him for weeks."

"He's here," said Tyrees.

Fifteen

Yes, man's presumptuous journey into the stars has diminished his significance—perhaps denied it entirely. He gazes upon an intimation of infinity, a dark shadow dotted by the pitiful, cold light of a billion galaxies. He is incredulous. He stands on the edge of this terrible idea . . . and is afraid.

—From the captain's log of Forger

THE MORNING—LIKE all mornings ushered forth by Tercet—was a glory of color and a promise of painful fire. Shadows were capricious, blasted darkly into the burgundy sand for the time needed to take careful note, then blurred and faded when a second sight was taken. Logos, Eros, and Sentos shunted for positions on the low horizon, ducking behind one another like children moving at games in slow time. At special times in the year they snubbed each other, and three shadows were cast, but at this time they nudged and cuddled and slapped at each other like youngsters exploring, but afraid, of each others' mysterious touch. Even this early their heat dried the membranes of the nostrils, hinted of the kind of innocent power that would soon burn through the wings of a butterfly.

The streets of Luta were again almost deserted, its inhabitants already in the fields. As he walked, Tyrees noted—as he had years earlier—the rough craftsmanship the Tercians had developed with stone, it being the only building material in plentiful supply. A round, waist-high wall dominated the village (basically wheel shaped, with lanes for spokes) at its hub. The wall was surrounded symmetrically by slender-necked stone jars as high as a man's shoulder. A visitor would admire the relative smoothness and uniformity of the impressive circle, the careful pointing of its mortar, the heavy grace of the jars. He might remark that it was pleasant to think of a people so close to the brink of survival who would spend precious effort on communal decor—and he would be wrong. Tercians had two sources of water: spring-fed wells which were virtually emptied daily to irrigate the fields, and two or three heavy rainfalls a year. Every village had its stone cistern to collect the latter, as large in area as it could manage. Fine grout kept the water from vanishing into the sand, but it had to be ladled quickly into the jars because evaporation was swift.

Tyrees sat on the cistern wall and waited patiently, morosely. He wondered if the stone circle on the earth was an unconscious imitation of the now invisible circle of stars in the sky. Tercet was a nexus, and so was he. The dull red spokes of the narrow lanes came at him. He shook his head almost violently.

"You are—disturbed, Vitar?"

Tyrees started, but before he turned, he knew who was there. Only a Seer could have surprised him, even given his present mood.

"Kreat-mel. Thank you for coming."

Kreat-mel bowed deeply, and with a solemnity that would be suspicious in another kind of man, he held forth his cane in the palms of both hands. Though the small ceremony was young and occasion gave it rare practice, this was the homage paid by the Seers to their Vitar. Tyrees touched it.

"Do you remember me, Vitar? It has been a long time since the wonderful bird called *Condor,* and we exchanged few words."

"I remember you very well, Kreat-mel. I could not do otherwise, for Meta-sol spoke of you often and with high praise."

Since this was meant as the simple truth, and not polite flattery, Kreat-mel took it so—and was therefore flattered. A hint of color rose to his leathery cheeks.

Though he moved with the slow fluidity of a thick syrup as he sat beside Tyrees on the wall, age spoke from every inch of his body. What on other old men's faces were wrinkles or creases, were on his carved terrain. Aside from touches of white flax over his ears, he was hairless. There was no sign of missing or decayed teeth when he smiled, but they were a pale brown in color and translucent at the tips. His hands were bone and sinew, their fingernails only hard skin.

In fact, he reminded Tyrees of his old mentor. Physically, the similarities were the superfluous ones of age, for Meta-sol was a diminutive man and Kreat-mel was slender and tall and beardless. Their manner of speaking, however, was the same, and so was the wellspring that gave it birth, for their trained powers of mind had taken the same subtle bent. Their strength was not in force, but in a sensitivity that was as mysterious to Tyrees as anyone else. He had always seen himself as a hulking butcher, and Meta-sol as a delicate surgeon.

"You have come, Vitar, to seek out some blight?"

Kreat-mel put his question matter-of-factly. Tyrees answered in the same fashion.

"In a way. How did you know? Tell me what you have seen."

Like all Tercian Seers, Kreat-mel was blind, but neither man considered the question inappropriate. His sightless eyes lifted unblinkingly toward the growing sear of the tri-star above, and his nose twitched slightly, like a hound testing the air. Like a hound, he shook his head. On another man the actions would have been comic.

"Nothing, Vitar. Just . . . a sense of it. Sometimes very strong . . . for a long time now."

Tyrees nodded slowly, spoke slowly. "You felt it like you felt *my* presence yesterday? Like you feel the presence of any object without physically seeing it?"

Kreat-mel smiled. Shyly, but with rebuke in his tone, he said,

"You did not become a child of Meta-sol without knowing that words do not explain such things."

"Try. Tell me what you can."

Kreat-mel's sandaled foot scraped at the hard-packed sand below the wall. "I do not like to speak of things I do not understand. . . . I feel my powers weakening with my years, Vitar." He fell into silence, seemingly embarrassed. Tyrees said nothing, only waited patiently for him to resume.

"I . . . cannot deal with it. It steals upon me in my dreams. It poisons the taste of food on my tongue. I am thankful you are here at last, Vitar."

Again there was a silence as they sat in the building heat of the Tercian morning. Tyrees released the collar clasp of his cape, feeling a familiar but oppressive weight settle itself along with the heat on the backs of his shoulders.

Suddenly a small boy of three or four emerged from one of the spoking lanes, wielding a stick. He took no notice of the two men as he toddled along holding the stick, clackety-clack, against the wall of a house. An old man—perhaps the boy's grandfather—rounded a corner with a limp, obviously in pain and expending great effort to catch up to his charge. He finally took hold of one pudgy, dimpled arm in his gnarled hand before he noticed the Seer and his darkly clad companion. His mouth fell open as he gathered the child to him. Then, not in fear but in humble apology, he ducked his head repeatedly, like a bird ducking for seed. He scurried with his squirming burden out of sight; but since he could not take his eyes off the two men sitting on the wall, he did so backward.

"You say you do not speak of things you do not understand," said Tyrees with careful calm, "but you speak of my return to Tercet in *The Teraac*."

"Yes, Vitar. I wrote what I knew," said Kreat-mel in the small, gentle puffs of sound that reminded Tyrees of Meta-sol. A hint of bitterness peppered his words. "Nothing else may be written there, and I only am left to write."

"Then what did you know?"

Kreat-mel sighed. "When I returned, I knew that there was a

presence here, one that was not within my sight before you took us to the hidden stars. I knew that it was growing. I knew that it was . . . destructive. I knew also that the time would come when you must meet it.''

"Why didn't you have the Emissary message me?"

Kreat-mel nodded. "You would have come, Vitar. This I know also. But what could you do then? You would listen to an old Seer whose powers are waning. You would seek it out, but you would not know whether to believe. That alone would make you . . . vulnerable.''

Tyrees felt beads of perspiration spring onto his forehead. He bent his head downward, away from the beautiful, deadly light. "You believed that I might be attacked in some way?''

Another nod. "Or you would fail. I could not help you beyond what I say now. I do not possess your strength.'' Kreat-mel turned his unlit eyes to Tyrees. "I hope that no man does. But now you are . . . armed. Now you *know*.''

Tyrees knew that Kreat-mel considered the threat to be localized, a hideous aberration, but one restricted to Tercet. He saw no point in telling the man that his caution helped to kill other Seers. He was also aware that Kreat-mel was canonizing him, giving him a level of awareness beyond his capacities simply because the Seer assumed that his Vitar would ultimately know of this man's presence just because he existed. His frustration grew.

"You must help me, Kreat-mel.'' Tyrees heaved himself off the wall and threw his cape into a crumpled heap on the ground. His voice was a hiss. The Seer registered his surprise with a delicate fluttering of fingers under the knob of his cane. "Unless I learn more about this man, he will destroy me! Do you *understand*.'' Kreat-mel's blank eyes widened like a child's. "Even then . . .'' Tyrees's voice trailed off. He stared at his cape; its soft black shimmers seemed to entrance him. "I am only a man,'' he said quietly. "Tell me what you can. Tell me how this *thing* feels. Tell me what you *don't* know.''

Kreat-mel's shoulders bowed. His head went slowly from

side to side like some great animal in pain. "It is . . . as I thought," he said. "When my *Vitar* is afraid . . ." He left the sentence unfinished.

The indifferent light of the Tercian sky was now layering down, dropping folds of oppressive, dry heat upon them. The sharp outlines of things an hour earlier were now blurred, melting into softer shapes under the burning spell of the tri-star. Tyrees stood staring sullenly at the black heap of his cape on the ground. He was remembering that he had done this once before, flinging his cape into the blood-dull sand when Bolla came to tell him that he and Tercet were marked for destruction.

"I, too, am afraid, Vitar." The puffs of sound from Kreat-mel were softer too—ghosts of sound, bubbles rising out of the heat. "And I am an old man who should not expect so much . . . benison from time." His shoulders lifted a notch. "You came here to challenge it . . . and you are afraid for much more than yourself. I must give what I can."

Kreat-mel took his cane and drew a circle in the earth between his feet. It was perfect in its roundness. "We all see in different ways," he said, "and one way alone is a dim path. That is why the dispersal of the community of Seers so saddens me—though I know it is only to strengthen the community in time, that you have made it so." Beside the circle he drew a series of jagged lines, not unlike the spiky patterns produced by a machine that records the layered asymmetry of brain waves. "My way of seeing is through the shapes of sounds."

Tyrees nodded, for there were echoes of his perception of the time track in this. Kreat-mel could not see the nod, but he knew it had taken place. "The circle—though never wholly closed, as this is—is what I see when many notes sound in harmony, when many efforts are bonded in a common goal, when the whole is greater than the sum of its parts. There is a chord then. Pure. Singular. The separate sounds become one." Kreat-mel paused for a moment to move his head from side to side again in that peculiar, lowing motion.

"I think I understand," said Tyrees. "The Gathering."

"Yes. That is when the circle is closest to being closed, and the harmony is . . . almost perfect."

Tyrees had participated in only one Gathering of the Seers, the one that proclaimed him the Seer of Seers, yet another of his many names. He had been awed by their concerted power, though he had not been able to distinguish how much of it had been his own. He knew others—certainly Meta-sol—could.

"The other shape is like this." Kreat-mel thrust at the jagged lines with his cane. "It is . . . an alien sound, and when it meets the other . . ." Kreat-mel extended the spikes so that each pierced the circle; then he passed his cane back and forth until the circle was all but obliterated. "Then there is only discord, a shriek of pain."

Kreat-mel mused over the marks in the earth for a time—before Tyrees took a single step and ground them under his boot.

"Or so it is that I see," said the old Tercian. "But I do not *understand* what I see. Can this come from a single *man?*"

Tyrees placed a hand on his shoulder. When he did so, he felt cords of muscle firm and tighten, and a quickening in blood flow. The gaunt chin lifted. Tyrees knew that the venerable Seer sensed portent and was beginning to be alarmed once more. He put his question with deliberate calm, knowing that it would not fool his listener.

"Who is Uni-shad?"

Kreat-mel frowned his confusion. "Uni-shad?"

"Yes. Is he not a Seer?"

Kreat-mel rose from the wall. "He is . . . *was* . . . perhaps. You think he is the . . . source, Vitar? It does not seem possible!"

"Tell me all you know about him. Why didn't he come with the rest of us? Why didn't Meta-sol try to save him when we thought Tercet might be destroyed?"

Kreat-mel was distracted. The swinging motion of his crevassed face returned. "Uni-shad," he muttered. "How could *he* become so—"

"Why couldn't he be the man?" asked Tyrees sharply.

"I would know his touch . . . would I not?"

"It's been almost seven years, Kreat-mel. And if he is the one, he's . . . changed a great deal."

Kreat-mel nodded thoughtfully. "More than seven . . . more than ten. Uni-shad did not come to the last Gathering."

"I know. Tell me why."

"Because of *you,* Vitar—and because of other things. He had *power*—like yours."

"What do you mean?"

"His strength was greater than ours, yet much less than yours. He was like you in the *nature* of his sight. Forgive me, Vitar, but . . . its *intensity,* its *wildness . . . it always seemed to threaten escape from his own control.*"

Tyrees looked across the baking expanse of the cistern's shallow bowl. In its center the heat concentrated, sending up heady, hazy shimmers. In them he saw Meta-sol's face once again; once again it was heavy with concern, and so, as almost always, were the words. Caution . . . restraint . . . *control.* Meta-sol had always feared at the level of his blood what Pol-Nesol-Rast, his spiritual son, might become. Tyrees had never truly understood that until this moment.

"Can a Seer go *mad,* Kreat-mel? Can he become . . . some kind of prisoner—an addict—to his own powers?"

Kreat-mel considered the question carefully. "I do not know," he said. "No Seer in my experience has ever lost his reason. Our most sacred teachings rest upon the efficacy of the mind."

"And Uni-shad?"

"He was . . . different, as you are different, but never violent, never destructive. He was passionate . . . unstable, at the very worst. And he was always apart from the rest of us. We may have been at some fault in that."

Guilt was a starved and puny demon among the Seers, but

Tyrees thought he detected its thin shadow lurking between Kreat-mel's words.

"Why was he alone?"

Kreat-mel sighed. "I did not say he was alone. He was apart from *us*." He hunched over on his cane, looking even older. "He took a woman."

Tyrees whistled softly. Acolyte Seers—on Tercet—voluntarily blinded themselves in early adolescence; they submitted themselves to a harrowing, three-day ritual that involved staring into the scorching tri-star during the daylight hours. The other lifelong self-denial was celibacy. Neither sacrifice was made on moral grounds. They simply believed that physical sight and physical lust were the prime tempters, inhibiting the growth of the other senses and of the mind that was meant to tap and foster them.

"He defied our efforts to dissuade him," said Kreat-mel, "and withdrew from the Seer community in anger. After a time of waiting—we hoped he would learn from his isolation and return to us—we shunned him . . . then ignored him. Even the people of his own village turned away from him, for his bond with the woman was . . . a duality, not a triad. One day he left the village and moved into the desert with his woman." Kreat-mel's voice wound sadly away with the stir of hot fuzzy air wafting up from the earth and the stone around them.

"If he was going to break from the Seers, why not into a triad instead of a—"

"A *marriage?* That is your name for it, is it not? I do not know, Vitar. But marriage is . . . not natural here, more rare than the falling of rain. We believe that if one is not a Seer, *three* fibers of the human personality are needed to make a strong weave." Here, Kreat-mel "looked" up at the tri-star. "Passion. Reason. The senses. When one is lacking . . ." He sniffed his dismissal of the thought. "Perhaps Uni-shad could find no other to join them. Perhaps he *preferred* marriage."

"So . . . he cut himself off. From the community of Seers and from the Learning."

"Yes. And we did not stay his knife . . . except for Meta-sol. He said to us that Uni-shad's powers were too . . . valuable to foresake, that they should not be discarded. He traveled often into the desert to speak to him, and to summon him to the Gatherings. Even after Uni-shad's woman died in childbirth he managed to do so, though the man was bitter.''

"But he wouldn't come to *my* gathering."

"He would not. Meta-sol told us that Uni-shad was angry. We could embrace an alien from the hidden stars, a man ignorant and scornful of our customs, yet we rejected *him* because he could not accept some of those same customs out of intimate knowledge. He sent Meta-sol away—and cursed us.''

A curse, Tyrees thought. One with some justice behind it. He stooped to pick up his cape, remembering his own curses thrown at the Regnum, the Chairman . . . the Cadre—when they had denied him *his* freedom. Had Uni-shad less cause? He could no longer sell himself the notion of evil unalloyed. And Uni-shad had lost a woman he loved . . . perhaps a woman like Shaamlik, a beautiful woman whose beautiful face became a mask of death.

Tyrees began to walk slowly around the low stone wall of the cistern. He trailed his fingers indolently along its top as he went, not unlike the little boy with the stick. When he had completed half the circle, he paused to look across the giant's flat kettle of heat at the bowed figure of Kreat-mel, who remained as he was, seated and unmoving. Then he continued round the circle, trailing his cape from one hand, tracing the wall with the other. By the time he returned to Kreat-mel, his walk had the look of a man passing through a dream.

"Tell me how to find him," he said.

Sixteen

"We are condemned to be free." These are the words of those of wisdom and prideful bitterness. Even wiser men claim that knowledge alone is our curse. Those who truly know say that simple consciousness is enough. So be it.

—The Sayings of Meta-sol

BECAUSE KREAT-MEL WOULD have it no other way, they went into the desert together. The heat was no greater. It was the land that was different. A narrow band ran along Tercet's equator, over which the sky squeezed a few precious inches of rain each year. Rainfall diminished with distance from the equator, until the cold but dessicated poles were reached.

There were many varieties of small animals on Tercet (some introduced by the original colonists), but the only beast of burden was man. He was the largest that the dry environment would tolerate—and only then if the will to survive were strong and the effort communal. When contact had been reestablished with the galaxy behind the black hole, the Seers had forbidden the resurrection of machines, knowing that such a change would impact upon their delicate culture in unpredictable ways. They would go slowly, from arm's length observation to cautious trial, before risking damage to the course of the Learning.

The terrain through which Kreat-mel and Tyrees trudged painted them with heavy brush strokes upon itself, for their very size and motion were gross, and therefore conspicuous. The red of the earth deepened and darkened here, diminishing the faltering attempts of other colors as it did life itself— though both had a discreet presence in tentative, unobtrusive forms, as if blatancy would bring death. Often the landscape would seem literally that—a stark, surreal painting of light and sand and sharp-edged rock in which the artist, seeking a hard simplicity, had omitted shadows: this when the three suns were some distance apart. The effect was disconcerting, for the senses of distance and dimension were distorted, and the traveler came suddenly upon objects he had thought to be at distance, or walked for an eternity toward a rock that was a mountain. Baking in the furnace of the tri-star, the reality of this landscape was harsh and uncertain, illusory and uncompromising.

With the curse of sight, Tyrees felt much more of this than his companion. Kreat-mel's only real handicap was his slowness afoot; Tyrees could not decide if this were a result of his blindness or his age, but it could have been neither. Haste was not inspired by Tercet or its Seers.

As they walked, words passed between them at long intervals like the passings of a shared burden.

"How long will this take, Kreat-mel?"

"Several days, Vitar. I do not know with precision where Uni-shad lives, but we will know that when we are nearer."

"Because we will sense *him,* or he *us?*"

"One or the other," said Kreat-mel negligently.

The difference seemed of little consequence to him. One of the "differences" between Tyrees and his Seers was their stoicism, their "what will be, will be" attitude—this in spite of their dedication to work toward certain goals.

"How do you know the way?"

"I sense it. I have been in Uni-shad's village, and I have Meta-sol's words to follow thereafter."

Tyrees shook his head silently. He, more than any non-

Tercian, had experience enough not to doubt—and he had his own powers—yet their blind wizardry never ceased to amaze him. Notions of the supernatural—magic—were anathema to him, as they were to the Seers; but "science," as it was hitherto known, could explain little of the Learning. The Seers did not measure or calculate. They saw.

"What . . . what paths do you follow?"

"I see lines. Do you not? They . . . pull, if I choose them."

The magnetic field of the planet? Perhaps. A skill not all of the Seers shared. That was the point of the community of Seers: to pool their abilities, to constantly add to the total, to the knowledge recorded in *The Teraac*. This was Tyrees's musing as he matched his pace to Kreat-mel's, so he was startled by his question.

"Vitar. Forgive me. Why do you not write for *The Teraac?* You have much to tell us. Our understanding would not be sufficient, perhaps, but we must be able to see *your* path. For the future."

They walked for a long time before Tyrees answered, though Kreat-mel showed no impatience. "I've given that question almost no conscious thought," he said, "but I have a feeling it has been with me a long time anyway." His tone was confessional, and it surprised even him—until he realized that he was speaking as he would have to Meta-sol, had his old mentor managed to outlive Tyrees's stubborn and (so he thought) secret fears. "I have to say that it's because I'm so unsure of things . . . of my 'sight,' certainly, and of where it might lead me . . . of my *self,* I suppose. How can I advise others?"

Kreat-mel nodded absently, as if he had just been informed of the time of day. His pace remained as ever, steady and calm, though he shifted the small pack on his back to a more comfortable position.

"You are first among Seers, Vitar. But though among Seers, you are first a man."

This was so like Meta-sol that pain plunged into Tyrees's chest like a knife, but he said nothing. Kreat-mel plodded on silently too—he had said all he wished to say.

With twilight—long and lingering on Tercet, as the three suns dawdled on the horizon—came spectacular plays of color. The light was passing through the thickest layer of atmosphere, three diffuse auras slanting into the airborne dust, the reds of the sand, the darks of the rocks. The bloody Eros was last to set, so her light and the sand bled together, erasing the horizon for a time, rendering a strange land into an impossible one, a place where walking men did not belong.

In the last of this eerie light the two men found some shelter from the sometimes fitful winds in a cluster of hovering boulders. They ate some dried grain cakes in silence. They sipped precious water. In silence they watched the rising of the black hole in the night sky. Kreat-mel watched from the tunnel of his memory, Tyrees from the here and now—but they saw the same thing.

Seventeen

Ye point a trembling finger at thine enemies. All are but masks of the real one—the one too terrible to uncloak. Know that ye have but one true Enemy. Ye may think that His color is the black of nothingness, and that His name is Death. This is wrong. Know that His true name is Time.

—The Teraac

THE FOLLOWING DAY was much the same: Walking at Kreat-mel's slow pace through the clear, burning light of the desert, exchanging words to an even slower rhythm that belonged to Tyrees. The walk and the talk, the heat and the light and the loneliness, gradually formed a bond that was easy and deep.

Somewhere along their way on the third day, Tyrees came to realize that he had had many fathers, and that Kreat-mel was yet another. His natural father had died when Tyrees was three, and he was a haunting ghost almost beyond the capture of memory. His glamorous grandfather, the Cadre Proctor, had taken him under his steely wing and became such an object of worship to the child that no "father" could survive it unblemished. Tyrees hated him in the end, for molding him dispassionately into a Cadre robot—until Bolla told him that Petr Tyrees was murdered because he had tried to protect his rebel grandson. Then there was Meta-sol, who—Tyrees had realized too late—was much more than a teacher. And Bolla. Bolla had always been there. Did the fat old man feel long ago as *he* finally did? That Tyrees was his "son"? Or was it—once again—too late.

He watched Kreat-mel's unfaltering gait as they trod again into the surreal Tercian twilight, and saw for the first time how much these men had given him, and how little they had, like true fathers, expected—or received—in return. For the first time in his adult life he felt like a lucky man. He was no longer young, but he *felt* young. And cared for. And protected.

"Kreat-mel?"

The old Tercian heard something rare veined into the calling of his name, for he stopped his remorseless tread and began to turn toward Tyrees. But something froze his turn abruptly. His head snapped up, then a hand.

"Wait."

Tyrees looked about him, seeing nothing but the deep, bleeding reds of Eros and the sand. "What's wrong?"

"I hear it," whispered Kreat-mel. "It grows stronger. Reach out with me. . . . Help me!"

Tyrees used his fear like a rapier, viciously swiping away the mode controlled by his normal senses. His mind became a black slate, a different awareness searching for marks that could be drawn upon its surface. At first there was nothing . . . nothing but a pale disk of light that he knew to be Kreat-mel. He pulled it to a higher brightness, expanded it, rode outward with its light. Then he heard it.

It sounded at first like a wasp's buzz—pesky and irritating, but almost subliminal. Quickly it grew in volume and mounted in pitch to a high whine. Tyrees was no longer the resident of a physical husk; he was the energy that sustained a white-lit disk of awareness that was not his alone, but under his control; he was master of a tenuous and fragile bulb of knowing that was threatened by a sound spear of entropic evil. He was an adjunct of Kreat-mel, and Kreat-mel was a soft chime of music, a dim sphere of light that faltered, hinted of dissolution into dischord and shadow with the piercing onslaught of an ever rising and jagged-edged screech.

With a strength fed by panic, Tyrees let flow his energy into a defensive resistance, a hardening of the bulb's tender, trembling skin. The sound was now shrill, a focused rasp, a penetrating, raping thrust at an infinitely small point in the bubble membrane that held in the light. He was just beginning— a puny child fumbling, gaping at his first experience of brutal violation—to pull his strength to that point, when the skin broke.

From somewhere far away came another sound. A squeak of whimpering. Pitiful . . . weak . . . lost . . . hopeless. With indignant outrage Tyrees flung everything between that note of dying and the horrible breach in the bubble's membrane.

When stars collide, there must be a sound. There must be a spatter of light through darkness, stark and random. So it was. After a time that knows no measure, Tyrees felt grains of sand shuffling between his fingers. He could feel his eyelids burning, too, but that was all. His mind reached for other awarenesses as a parched man would reach for water, but there was nothing else. Sand gritting between clawing fingers. Searing heat blistering his eyelids. His mind drew inward then. First it searched for will—to open his eyes, perhaps; there was none. Next it sought memory—who he was, where he was; there was none. He was only fingers and eyelids, sand and burning. Mothlike, his mind flitted between the two.

After a time the moth began to tire. Its wings beat back and forth ever more desperately, and the space between the fingers and the eyelids was an abyss. Because it could do nothing else, because it could not accept the abyss, the spent moth finally settled upon the fingers.

They clawed. Slowly, ceaselessly, the fingers flexed and clutched, flexed and clutched. Sand was embedded deeply under the nails, flayed at raw flesh in the tips and between the knuckles. This much could be known. A quivering moth, the mind did all it could do—cling to the sensations from the fingers.

Suddenly the harsh but bearable abrasions felt by the fingertips were shot with excruciating pain. The mind cringed. The clawing continued, but now spasmodically. The mind, even in its cringing, celebrated the change. The pain was a tide, moving rhythmically, with each surge mounting higher, and the mind became aware of an arm, then a shoulder, then a pulse of blood pounding in counterpoint at the base of the skull.

The surges of pain from the clutching fingers gradually became explosive—so much so that the whole body suddenly came alive with it, and the moth disappeared.

Tyrees moaned and opened his eyes. They were hot coals suspended in his skull. It was mid-morning. He was on his back, but was able to roll away from the direct glare. He could not see clearly, but he could make out near his right side a trench in the sand more than a foot deep; it exposed a corrugated bottom of flinty rock. He stared at it stupidly for a long time before he connected it with the pain. Struggling to an elbow, he pulled his right hand from under him and squinted at it. The crusted aggregate on the ends of his fingers was the same black-red color as the sand—the color of dead blood— but much of it *was* sand. Some healthy blood seeped sluggishly through. It was the white of bone gleaming out of the caking of his longest finger that sent waves of nausea through him.

Clutching the hand to his chest, he tried to stand, but his eyes delivered only a swimming pattern of things in the distance, adding to the nausea. Even his knees refused to take his crushing weight. He fell back on his rump.

Only then did he notice the figure stretched beside him in the sand. He had to come to all fours and creep forward, fighting for sight through the flames in his eyes before its face took on some clarity. He had to think for a while before he could put Kreat-mel's name to it. Then he brought his good hand to his own face and sobbed.

The Seers preached and the Seers taught—control. Control was their god and they worshiped him, made sacrifices to him, aspired to his perfection. Tyrees was the first among Seers, so he wept for the death of his god as well as for Kreat-mel. And he wept at the loss of another father.

The sound of his weeping was a small thing in the Tercian desert, smaller even than the dark rub of his figure on the merciless landscape which was so brilliantly ablaze with the clarity of its indifferent light. The sound died slowly, was slowly swallowed by the light and the heat.

The man who finally rose from the sand, the skin of his face sun-blasted like that of a young Seer-to-be after the Purging, was not the same man who had trudged into the shadows of the mauve twilight the day before. He was not a *man* at all, for there was little consciousness; consciousness would have required that he bury Kreat-mel to protect him from scavengers, would have demanded that he stoop to pick up the water and the food. Instead, some unfathomable impulse led him on unsteady feet deeper into the desert.

His eyes delivered only distorted, freakish images—and pain—from a distance, so they were lowered, half closed, to the ground at his feet. Sometimes they were closed completely, though he continued to walk into the desert.

He walked through that day and into the night. His steps were uneven and faltering, but as ceaseless as a machine. He had spent much of his life—especially the last years—struggling to control the part of his mind that obeyed the commands of the primal helix. Now it controlled him.

For Tercet, that first night was very dark. The ring of the black hole was a wan halo, a dim wisp of light separating darkness from a darkness deeper yet. So was his mind. Yet it was not blind. It did not allow him to blunder into rocks or holes. The almost useless eyes were always closed now, but another sight was growing.

He walked into the second day, into the glorious purgatory of light and heat that was truly Tercet. But the power and the knowledge born of the cell, the mystical chemistry that lifted and set his feet safely through the sand, was infant-vulnerable in many ways. It could husband the resources at its command like a computer; it could balance the ecology of the body—especially this body—to the optimum. But it could not provide water.

In the mid-afternoon of the third day, when the heat was at its peak, Tyrees's automatic pace began to take on the spasmodic jerkiness of a comic toy. The inner membranes of his mouth and nostrils had been raked by the air into a papery dryness that was now invading his lungs. The feet became too heavy even for the most basic of life energies, and the conscious mind returned for a short time in the form of dizziness and dream and dementia—before he fell into merciful darkness.

Eighteen

What is to fear? Things that make sounds in the night? There is only death, after all.

—Uni-shad

FIRST THERE WAS oblivion, then dreams—horrible dreams. Shaamlik's mask loomed toward him out of the darkness. It had no eyes. Though he knew something terrible was festering behind it, he kept reaching out to pull it away. It eluded him for a time, until he dove and hooked two fingers into the sockets of its eyes. There was a scream as it began to come away, but he kept pulling at it, pain creeping up his arm from the fingers. It pealed slowly back like a false skin, and as it gave, the scream intensified, changed pitch until it was the same, jagged, tearing sound that had found him in the desert.

At the moment the mask came away he closed his eyes so he would not see. But the sound went on, inexorably, as he waited in terror, eyes closed, for his mind to shatter like a sheet of vibrating glass.

Then, out of no source that he could discern, came a wash of balm. It flooded over him, salved him, transformed pain into the peaceful pleasure of stroking fingers on aching muscle. Cool water flowed over parched skin, down his burning throat.

He slept, and the dreams did not return. When he awoke, he was not certain of his wakefulness, for his eyes would not open. He found himself reluctant to attempt to open them. A cool, damp cloth passed tenderly over his forehead and cheeks, more tenderly over his eyelids.

"There now . . . there now. Feels good, doesn't it?"

A woman's voice, a wonderful, soft, compassionate voice. It gave him the courage to open his eyes. He could make out the shadowed image of her face—young, broad of brow, skin of dark cream—and knew that he was in a darkened room which did not fully account for his dim vision.

"You . . . Where am I?" The sound of water, dripping.

"You're here. In the desert. You're going to be allright. Tell me your name." The cloth resumed its cool passage, now across his bare chest.

"My . . ."

"Name. What were you doing out here alone?"

Name? . . . Then it all came crashing down upon him with the force of an avalanche. Tyrees . . . Pol-Nesol-Rast . . . Vitar . . . Uni-shad! With a choked cry he struggled to rise, but her face swam in front of him and he almost blacked out.

"Easy now! . . . Easy . . . that's it. Relax. You're allright. Here. Drink."

He felt her shift closer to lift his head into the cradle of her arm, felt his cheek touch a breast through coarse fabric. He drank.

"There. That's better . . . not too much, now. Good."

He felt like a child again—a sick child being lovingly cared for, though he could not remember any of those conditions. He knew that he had not experienced all of them.

"Can you talk now? Can you tell me your name?" Her voice, like her face was young, yet it contained within it timbres of compassion and experience that were ageless. Or was this simply a voice that he needed, a construct of his blasted state? He pulled words out of his throat like so much gravel.

"My . . . name is . . . Radis."

"Good. You're feeling better." She eased his head back onto something soft. "The worst is behind you now."

The sound of water and the feel of cool cloth returned. He closed his eyes again, as much because of their failure to bring clarity as his fatigue. He wanted to see her better. But he drifted off with the feel of her fingers lingering on his skin.

This time as he slept the old modes of awareness—modes long etched deeply into mind-patterns of his own design—began to reassert themselves. He knew that he was suffering the effects of the tri-star, fatigue, and dehydration; that he had been rescued by the woman and was lying in the two-room, stone house that was everywhere on Tercet; that his eyes had been damaged, though he would have to be much healthier to judge the extent of that damage. He knew also that he would recover quickly. But what was this woman doing in the desert? Was she alone, as she appeared to be? Thoughts of Kreat-mel and the sound that found them in the mauve light of the desert stood in the distance like threatening storm clouds, but he would not allow them to approach—rest would not be possible then.

When he had tapped the resting mode as long as his body required, his eyes opened to a room dappled with chinks of light. He realized immediately that it had been darkened and that he had awoken in daylight. From outside he heard sounds of splashing water—sounds he had already come to associate with his rescuer. He confirmed what he already knew: that his sight was distorted at a distance, blurred at middle range, and only acceptable within the length of his arm. He tried to "see" and assess the damage to his lenses, but found that his powers of concentration were inadequate. He would have to be patient, wait until more of his health returned before he could call upon resources denied ordinary men.

He rolled his legs off the cot and sat upright before realizing that he was naked. Looking at himself, he saw that he had reverted somewhat to the state he had fallen to when he had become addicted to the time track just before the coup. Every bone was molded by his skin, though muscles corded over them. Without looking, he knew that the fingers of his right hand were healing quickly—all but the index, which would eventually become only bone with scar tissue at its tip. The nail, now only a nub of bluish black, would become a paper-thin membrane, even given his capacity to send it extra blood, for it was already too late. The memory of Kreat-mel's fingertips leapt into his mind, but he cut that off sharply. Both his body *and* his mind needed healing time.

He stood with difficulty, fighting off a not unpleasant dizziness. He could ignore the pain from his hand and his burned skin (in his present state, he no longer had the capacity to cut it off entirely), but not the weakness or the stiffness of his legs. Gingerly he made it to the door and opened it. The light hit him violently. He threw one forearm over his eyes with a gasp and groped for the door frame.

"Radis!"

She had called from her tiny garden. The white wall of light that had struck him had brought with it an image that was now burned into the backs of his eyes—the outline of a female form bent to the task of pouring water from a bucket. The form was without detail, solid and white; the background was dark and murky. She was half supporting, half pushing him back through the door in an instant; in another he was back on the cot and the door slammed closed.

The sound of water again. He felt the moist cloth fall over his eyes, watched the whiteness in his brain gradually die.

"I don't know how you were able to stand!" she exclaimed. "I wouldn't have left you! You've got to protect your eyes from the light. I know!"

Tyrees regained his composure quickly, enough to feel discomfited by his nakedness. He fumbled at the coarse blanket beneath him. She must have sensed it, for he felt another blanket thrown over him immediately. When she was lifting his injured hand free of it, he grasped her wrist.

"Please. I'm all right now. Who are you?"

He heard an intake of breath. He took it to be her surprise at his lucidness, the speed of his recovery.

"I am Cubus," she said, and briskly set about finishing her arrangements with her free hand. "We will talk later, though. You need rest . . . and perhaps some food? You've been taking only liquids. We can talk later."

Something in her manner of speaking struck him as curious. Something did not belong, but he could not identify it.

"We can talk now. I'm not delirious. You found me in the desert . . . somewhere near. What are you doing here?"

"I live here. . . . Yes, I found you almost within sight of the house. What are *you* doing here? You are not a Tercian."

"I am . . . a Cadre One."

She hesitated. "Oh! Like the Vitar was? A soldier?"

"Of a kind."

Without letting go of her wrist, he lifted the cloth with his other hand and opened his eyes. This close, he could see her quite clearly. She had beautifully smooth, dark skin, rich and glowing from her work outside. The hair was nondescript, short and spiky, as if cut negligently by the handful. Her features were regular and pleasant but unremarkable, except for a handsome forehead now softly creased with lines of concern. It was her eyes that were striking: impossibly large and round, with an unfleeting look of wonder and innocence. They were predominantly dark, but shifted subtly from color to color like the illusive Tercian twilight. They compelled one to look and enter deeper, layer by layer, to share her passive wonder. She was even younger than he had first assumed—early twenties at most. He released her wrist.

"Thank you for saving my life," he said quietly.

She smiled for the first time, and shrugged. "What else could I do? There you were."

"Nothing. You could have done nothing."

Her laugh had subtle layers, too, a laugh that found humor in unexpected places. "That may be true on your world. No one here would have let you die."

"I thank you in any case, Cubus. Why did you remove my clothes?"

"They are strange clothes," she said, "but such wonderful cloth. Do all of your people wear them?"

He shook his head. "They are a uniform. They identify me as a Cadre man."

"They needed to be washed. And your skin—it needed water. It drank like the sand. It drank a whole bucket, and my garden is jealous of you."

These ingenuous words—and the attitude behind them—told him why he had found her speech puzzling earlier. She spoke naturally, exclusively, in the first person, as any non-Tercian would. And she thought in those terms. She was not part of a triad. On Tercet only Seers were alone.

"Where is your family, Cubus?"

"I have no family," she said sternly, rising from the cot. "You must eat." She moved to the center of the room and stooped to lift up a trapdoor. Her movements were catlike, quick and lithe—so much so that he watched her more closely. The shapeless shift she wore took on some of her form as she turned and bent gracefully to climb down a ladder into the root cellar; it had soft curves and hard muscle.

She returned with a wooden bowl of flour and a kind of vegetable, all of which she had cradled in her arms; she had climbed the ladder easily, using only her bare feet. With one of these, she flipped the door over on its hinges, catching it before it slammed into the floor, and lowered it gently.

"You have remarkable balance, Cubus."

"Yes?" She smiled. "I am strong too. I carried you here . . . Radis." She spoke his name as if she enjoyed the sound of its strangeness. She stared at him for a moment before turning with the food to a table, and he wondered if he were the object of her curiosity simply because she lived alone.

Her hands moved deftly as she prepared the simple meal. As if no activity pleased her more, she hummed without self-consciousness. The sounds had no melody, but they were pure and natural and vaguely comforting to the man on the cot, who had known little feminine domesticity in his life.

When she was finished at the table, she brought the bowl and a crude metal spoon to his cot and sat on its edge. He struggled to a sitting position against the wall and reached for the bowl, but she stayed his hand with hers.

"I will feed you, Radis." Her tone allowed no compromise. He found himself nodding and opening his mouth to the spoon. He found himself willing to trust, happy to be under her care.

The pasty, lumpy mixture was unsightly, but delicious. Heavily spiced and with an herbal odor, it lifted his spirits and made his body come alive again. They did not speak through the meal, but she seemed to take pleasure from his appetite. She spooned deliberately, dark eyes wide, with total absorption, until the bowl was empty.

"More?"

He shook his head.

"Please. It will only take a minute."

"No, thank you, Cubus. I can't remember tasting anything better than that. Or being served so well."

She blushed. The big, round eyes fell to her lap. One hand went to her hair, fluttering there for a moment. Then she stood abruptly and brought the spoon and bowl back to the table. The room had become even darker, and when she moved away, he saw her only dimly, a ghostly figure of a woman who moved with lithe grace on bare feet. She returned and leaned over him to pull a curtain away from a small window over his cot. She smelled of clean, warm earth. Soft, amber light flooded the room from another of Tercet's capriciously colored twilights. She knelt on the floor beside him and leaned on one arm, drawing her legs under her shift. In the tender light she looked very vulnerable, very lovely.

"You are from the hidden stars," she said. "Will you tell me about them?"

"All of them?" He smiled in spite of his cracked lips. "There are hundreds, Cubus, and they are all quite different."

"Oh . . . of course." She plucked at the hem of her rude dress, then slapped at it. "I hate being ignorant," she said bitterly. "All Tercians are ignorant."

"Why do you say that?"

Her voice was petulant. "Because they prefer to stay here. Don't you know that? The hidden stars . . . there must be so much to see and . . . there must be wonderful things to see!"

Tyrees felt strings pull across his chest. He let his head fall back against the wall and reached out to touch her cheek.

"Yes, Cubus. There *are* wonderful things . . . and terrible things too—things unknown to Tercet and better *left* unknown. Did you know that your world is looked upon as a holy place now? Many would trade places with you."

She pouted. "Yes, I know, but I do not understand why. Is it only because the Vitar came here and became a Seer?"

"No. It is because Tercet has seen and taken a new direction, even though it began a thousand years ago. Our species is flawed, Cubus, perhaps even self-destructive. We have an inestimable potential coupled with . . . with a death wish."

Cubus stared at him, eyes blown wide with fear and wonder and incredulity.

"But . . . but . . ."

"Tercet taught us the primary lesson: power gathered and exerted exclusively on the external plane simply increases our capacity to destroy. Everything. We augment our control over everything but *ourselves*. We are—and have always been— children playing with fire."

Cubus frowned. She ran the fingers of one hand through her unruly hair and shook her head. She looked sullenly up at Tyrees, the jaded adult scorning her unicorns.

"You mock me," she said. Tears formed at the corners of her large, hopeful eyes. Tyrees saw them, scorned them, loved them.

"You are young, Cubus."

"I am young, but I am not stupid!" she said angrily. "You sound like my father! I just want to see the things that are there to be seen! Why does that make me a monster?"

Tyrees was taken aback. Suddenly he realized what it was to trot out abstract truths—as poignant as they may be—and flaunt them at those whose experience was a shallow puddle compared to their intellect.

"No, it doesn't make you a monster. I'm sorry I preached at you. It's just that you should not be ashamed of your people. They produced the spiritual leaders of a galaxy; most feel 'ignorant' beside *them*."

"You are speaking only of our Seers, Radis. What about the rest of us? Are we to moon about in the desert when there are machines that fly between the stars?"

"Someday, if you really want to, you will visit the hidden stars, Cubus."

"*You* have already. You have seen many of them."

"Yes. It's part of my . . . job."

Her eyes, still filmed with tears, became enormous. "Will you help me? Please, will you help me get there?"

Tyrees couldn't look at her eyes. As a young man he had been a victim of his own innocence; but had he *ever* been *this* innocent?"

"I can't promise you that, Cubus."

She sniffled and drew the back of her wrist under her nose. Then, flashing at him a look that was both embarrassed and pleading, she rose quickly from the floor and went to the bucket to splash water on her face. She took her time, and said nothing, keeping her back to him. He saw the lines of disappointment, perhaps even hopelessness, falling down through her neck and into her shoulders. Like a child she gathered the loose shift together in the front to dry herself. Again he was reminded that the body underneath was not that of a child—nor that of an ordinary woman. It was indeed feminine, almost voluptuous, because the curves were bold, and even through the dull fog of his weakness he felt long- quiet stirrings; but the body also resonated strength. Again, the meld of soft curve and hard muscle.

Whether from this sight of an unusual woman in the dead quiet of loneliness and loss in the Tercian desert—loss he had not yet come to terms with—or from a sense of debt unpaid to one who had certainly saved his life, he changed his mind.

"Cubus."

She did not turn, but there was no reproach in her voice. "Do not apologize. I must make my own way—and I will, some day."

"I will help you," he said. "I didn't refuse you earlier because it wasn't possible, Cubus, but because I couldn't promise *when*."

She turned, her face bright with joy. "Oh . . . thank you! Thank you, Radis!" She ran to his cot with the speed and lightness of a cat. Falling on her knees once more, she clasped his hand in both of hers and held it against her. He could feel the cool dampness from the water still on her skin.

"I owe you much more than that. But remember, it may take some time."

"Oh, I will wait *years!* I will use the time to study about the galaxy. I will see the Emissary. I will—"

"It won't take years, Cubus."

Unless I am dead. The thought flitted through his mind like a bat through a dark cavern—unbidden and unwelcome, but soon gone. Still, it frightened him, and he actually winced.

"Oh," she said. "You are in pain?"

"No. Just weak. And tired."

She let go of his hand to touch his chest lightly with tender fingers. "Your skin is still like dried paper . . . one moment."

She rose once again and hurried to a cupboard from which she removed a small, heavy glass jug of clear oil and a mortar and pestle. With the latter she began to grind small rootlike fibers, something that had been a part of his meal because he recognized the rich, spicy odor.

As he watched her work, the room gradually took on a darker, dimmer shade of color, and he knew that one of the suns had set. By the time she was finished, his damaged eyes could only render her as a whitish image, a wraith concocting a potion. Oils and unguents, herbs and spices. The rasp of the pestle, the gurgle of a heavy liquid poured, the balming sound of her hum. She returned bearing the same bowl from which she had fed him, now full of the clear oil, but dense with multicolored specks in suspension. The smell became pungent —powerful, strange, but not unpleasant. She knelt once more, placing the bowl on the floor.

"What is that, Cubus?"

"A healing mixture," she giggled, the girl in the young woman emerging again momentarily. "A great secret taught me by my father."

"For victims of the desert?"

"Yes . . . and other things," she said, resuming the stern mother voice of earlier. "Lay back."

Again he obeyed without protest, pushing his shoulders down the wall until he was lying flat on the cot. She dipped both hands into the bowl and brought them dripping onto his chest. The odor suddenly became overwhelming, almost stifling. His nostrils closed in a spasm and his good hand came up to push her hands away.

"Relax, Radis," she said brusquely. Her strong fingers pushed the warm oil over his skin. "Breathe deeply and the smell won't bother you . . . breathe . . . that's right."

She dipped her hands again. His skin was absorbing the oil quickly, becoming slippery and yielding. As she had promised, the odor, though still pervasive, ceased to be cloying. As she worked, she, too, was breathing deeply. Soon his eyes closed, and without a sense of passage he floated into a thick, focused dream woven with the feel of her fingers and a headiness augmented each time he filled his lungs.

Visually there was nothing—a blind miasma, frightening, decadent. His body was a sensual net that caught only pleasure, each strand craving, demanding, parched for indulgence. He snake-slipped through smooth, heavy oils; his nostrils inhaled a concupiscent scent of excruciating allure; sweetness invaded his tongue. Pervading it all was the call of a siren, a rich hum of irresistible temptation, of apocalyptic promise.

He was a phallus. His whole being was tumescent. He sought only for the explosion of ecstasy for which he had that being.

The sensations were so powerful, so wild, that the underlay of fear welled up. With hooked fingers he clawed at his face, trying to find a place for self again. Nothing changed. Below, he was hardened to the verge of pain. His hands left his face to reach for his groin, where the heat was volcanic.

But other hands were already there. He shook with a tremor of excitement so violent that some mechanism came into play. His eyes opened. A kind of charged awareness returned. Cubus was rising from the floor, releasing him. Her luminous eyes, now deepest violet like the desert twilight, were glazed over with something akin to the veil of heat that tortured him—but her actions betrayed no immediacy.

Slowly, slowly—because she held herself on the far side of the membrane that pulsed between pain and pleasure, the side remote from his entrapment—she pulled her shift over her head. Even as he was, he took in with some detachment the beauty of her body—beauty that just missed visiting her face. Her breasts were strong, hard muscle sheathed in her soft skin of dark cream. Her nipples were high and erect. He moaned softly.

As she stood over him, her eyes, shading darker, met his. He could only stare back into those violet depths and tremble. She smiled then, a smile of infinite knowledge, and swung a confident leg smoothly up and over the cot to mount him.

He convulsed. But she, still on the far side of the membrane, settled on him slowly, drinking him in deliberately, not allowing him a quick release. Nevertheless, the pressure of her thighs on his, the oily ream of entry, brought him close to delirium. She waited until he calmed, waited until she could move without triggering his eruption. Then she milked their pleasure.

His release was cataclysmic. He called out like a man being pulled violently—at the last moment—from quicksand. The sound of his climax triggered hers, and she rode him from a gallop into a leap of soaring pleasure, although he was already too spent to register it.

An empty shell, thoughtless and sated into indolence, he lay in her arms through the Tercian night. They did not speak, though at times he could hear the sound of her humming, a sound so soft and natural that, like the sound of air in leaves, it seemed to vanish in the moment of notice.

When light began to leak back into the room, slowly bringing objects out of the darkness and back into a tentative reality, he found he could speak to her again.

"You said the oil was for healing."

Her fingers stroked his hairless scalp. This was the first time that he noted that it was gone. Perhaps it lay beside Kreat-mel.

"Was it not?"

He had nothing to say to this. He watched the light thicken and glow on the curve of her haunch. "It could be dangerous. That much I know, though it affected you less than me."

She licked his ear. "You took it into your skin. I only breathed it. Besides, I am more used to it."

"You are very young to have knowledge of such a drug."

"Why, Radis? Everything we eat is a drug." She smiled down at him. "And I am older than you think."

"How old is that?"

"You are old because you have seen much, done much. In that way I am very young. Like all Tercians I am very young because they force me to hide with them behind the black hole."

There was bitterness in her voice, but she lowered his head gently before springing gracefully from the cot. He noted that one arm took her full weight with ease as she vaulted over him to the floor. She walked on light feet into the semidarkness to the table. Unquivering, her buttocks were sculpted out of soft, dark marble. He could not take his eyes from her form as she moved about preparing food. There was nothing of the drug left in him; now he yearned for her in his mind rather than his body.

"I do feel much stronger," he called to her.

As he wanted, she turned and smiled. "Good. How are your eyes?"

"Not much better, but there is no pain." He pulled himself back to his sitting position against the wall. He blinked—then, convulsively, his hands went to his eyes. She saw the movement.

"Oh! Those clear things over your eyes? One must have come

out when you were in the desert. I took the other out myself, when I realized it was there. Do they help you see?''

"Uh, yes . . . but I need them only for very long distances.''

"Then you shouldn't wear them,'' she said coyly. "They change the color of your eyes . . . and you have wonderful eyes—magician's eyes.''

This unsettled him. He was usually intolerant of people who tried to compliment him—but this unfathomable woman melted all his rules and habits and inclinations into slag. He searched for something to say.

"In a day or so I'll be good enough to travel. You'll have one less burden.''

She had just picked up a knife, but stopped with it raised above a pale green, lettucelike vegetable. It came down with a slam before she responded.

"Then you will belong to me—my burden—until then.''

Again he was taken aback. "I won't forget my promise, Cubus.''

She lowered her knife and looked at him solemnly. "No. I don't think you will, Radis. You are a stranger from the hidden stars. I do not know you, but I trust you.''

"Why?''

She came back to the cot and retrieved her shift from the floor. "Because we are alike, you and I. This much I know.'' She slipped the rough garment over her head and down to her calves in an easy motion, a door closing on his eyes.

"*How* are we alike?''

"In many ways, but only one is important. We are both alone.''

He stared at her hard, a look that very few had been able to return in the last few years. She did. There was nothing now of the ingenuous girl with the water bucket. Tyrees would not deny his aloneness to himself, but he was affronted nevertheless.

"Oh? And how do you know this?''

She shrugged, as if it were a given. "By things you said when you were still delirious. By the way you keep close thoughts to yourself—you are a man of secrets. . . . And by the way you make love.''

His answer was a defensive reflex proving what she said. ''Was it me or the *drug* that made love?''

She turned brusquely and swept the vegetables into a bowl. ''I cannot speak for you,'' she said angrily, ''but the mixture does not choose my lovers for me.'' The bowl hit the table with a bang.

He said nothing. She grabbed the water bucket, threw open the door, and marched out. He winced at the sudden light of the full-blown sunrise. From outside came the sound of a hand pump, furiously worked. He fumbled out of the cot to his feet and stood still for a moment, assessing his strength and balance. He felt weak and disoriented, but no longer sick. On a low counter under a shuttered window he saw a neat pile of black cloth. He walked gingerly over to pick it up. It was his uniform—neatly folded, carefully washed. Carefully washing anything but one's body on Tercet was almost a sacrilege. He looked at it dumbly for some time before struggling into it, leaving the collar open and ignoring the cape. His boots, polished to a high shine, were under the cot. He had them on when she returned, carefully closing out the light behind her.

Glancing at him with studied composure, she said, ''You do look better. We will eat soon. You will want some tea first.'' She swung the bucket onto the table and was reaching for a ladle when he took her hand.

''Cubus. Please . . . I want to talk to you.'' He led her back to the cot and they sat, but he kept her hand.

''I'm sorry for what I said.'' Her eyes filled the room again, and the guileless young girl returned. ''You were right. I am alone. I don't speak of . . . of personal things easily. You are alone too . . . but you have more . . . courage, I guess. You take risks.''

She shook her head. ''No. No, no. I have nothing to lose. At least . . . I *had* nothing.''

''What do you mean?''

"You gave me—hope. . . . Oh!" She smiled in self-derision. "Perhaps that is what you meant by 'risk'?"

"Hope of leaving Tercet, of seeing the galaxy? That is no longer a hope, Cubus. You *will* see it."

"That, yes. But not just that. I hoped that you . . ." She looked down at their clasped hands. "Would love me. I know I could love you."

Tyrees was so startled that he dropped her hand and stood. He did not know if he trembled because of his state of health or her words.

"You don't know me," he said.

She giggled. "We just talked about that, and you became angry."

He frowned and sat again. "Allright. Secrets—you talked about secrets. You are young, beautiful, intelligent. You have known men intimately—perhaps many. Yet you live alone here on the desert. Why?"

Without looking at him, she returned her hand to his. "The village is less than a day's walk," she said quietly.

"Answer my question, Cubus."

She played with his fingers, as if fascinated with their slenderness and suggestion of hidden strength. "I am not beautiful," she said with conviction.

"Answer my question."

"At first," she said, almost whispering, "there were some men. And I wanted them, but they didn't want me. Later, I didn't want *them*. You are the first since my father died."

"You said I reminded you of your father."

"Yes. I will tell you of that. I will tell you anything you want to know, Radis. My secrets are only important to *me*. Most of them are not even secrets—except to you."

Still, she would not look up at him. Now, both her hands were caressing his fingers. Suddenly, her use of his false name appalled him. But if he were to deny it, he didn't know which of the others to confess to.

"I am . . . a soldier," he said. "Most of my secrets would not concern you."

"Tell me a small one then," she said, pulling his hand against her, "and I will answer all your questions. I *want* to tell you about me!"

"I'll tell you what I can."

"What does *that* mean?" she asked suspiciously, now looking up at him, eyes full and vulnerable. "*I* make no conditions."

"I have to, Cubus. Some of it may harm others—even you."

"Oh. Yes . . . you're a soldier. I'm sorry. This is all strange to me. Can you tell me why you came here? Why you were dying on the desert?"

"Yes . . . some of it." He did not want to think of his ugly hunt, or of his quarry. "I came looking for a man. A murderer."

Her hands tightened on his. "You . . . He attacked you? Here in the desert? Is that why—"

"Yes."

"Then . . . he was a murderer? Why didn't he kill you? You were helpless when I found you!"

Tyrees considered the question for the first time. He had to shake his head. "I don't know."

"Well," she said. Her lips drew back from her teeth with hatred. "He had better not come here. I would know he was near. I would kill him myself." She looked at him defiantly. "I could, you know. I am quick, and I am very strong. He would not expect it in a woman. You need not be afraid *here*."

I would know he is near. His mouth went dry. Suddenly, many things made sense.

"Cubus. *You know the Learning, don't you?*"

She looked at him sharply, then scowled. "Some. Not *The Teraac*—that is nonsense. Some of the disciplines." She pushed his hand from her lap and stood, hands on hips. "You find it repulsive in a woman? Like the others? Are you afraid of me too?"

"Who taught you? No Tercian Seer would—"

"My father, Uni-shad."

Nineteen

Such is the covenant of the Seer. To be blind that he may see.

—The Teraac

"AND YOUR MOTHER died when you were born?"

"Yes. For the rest of his life my father believed he was responsible for her death. His pride would not permit him to seek the help of the birthing triad in the village. I was born—upside down, Radis. Feet first."

Tyrees had long ago come to curse his own beginnings. Hers were worse. Upside down. The mother dying. A twisted heritage of guilt. Alone.

"All this because he rejected the triad? He was a *Seer*, after all."

Cubus went to the dry sink to scour their bowls with red sand. She had been speaking during the last hour as if out of a dream—passionless, without spirit, almost indifferently, assuming from a lesson of twenty years that her beginnings could have no impact on anything, anyone, but herself.

"Yes, he was a Seer. A man of great learning. Before he broke their stupid taboo and brought my mother into the desert, he was considered one of the greatest." She paused in her scouring to turn to him where he sat at the table. Her face was weary. "They were envious of him, you know, and he was even more gifted than they thought. He was too *free* for them to accept. He denied all custom for custom's sake. . . . But in the end they destroyed him. Or their *guilt* destroyed him. They will not destroy me."

"They ostracized *you* as well as your father? The people, I mean."

"Of course." She smiled bitterly. "But they were afraid of us too. I'm sure you don't know this, Radis, but Tercians are very superstitious. There is too great a distance between them and their Seers. Seers are made into gods here."

He knew all too well. "Yes, I know they revere the Seers—as they should. But . . . 'superstition'?"

"There is no other name for it. They toil. They spend themselves so that a few men can spend their whole lifetimes on the Learning. They witness what a Seer can do, and they do not really understand. Even in spite of the Seers themselves, they seek simple answers out of their ignorance. My father explained this to me. It was simplest for them to see my father as a sorcerer—and me as a witch. He was a Seer who must deny physical love, and he took a single partner; he denied the triad; he taught his daughter in the ways of a Seer; he did not follow *The Teraac*."

Cubus had been staring vacantly at the wall throughout this recitation—a litany of her father's sins. She knew them well, and her tone was a spit of scorn denying them all. "Some went further," she added, as if relishing their folly. "They said he took the Learning and twisted it for what must be evil purposes. He did not follow *The Teraac,* yet he had the Learning; therefore, he was a servant of the black hole, a priest of darkness who laughed at rules and customs and morality."

Out of the well of his own ancient regrets, out of his present fears, Tyrees felt something new take root in his soul—pity. It was so powerful, and he found it so amazing, that he was shocked by it at first.

"Surely the Seers did not tolerate such warped and malicious thinking, Cubus. I know many of them well."

She laughed. "Perhaps not as well as you think. They are not fools. Where would they be without their peoples' faith in them? I am certain that they knew the injustice, but lacked the courage to fight such ignorance. They were afraid of angering the people—so my father said."

So even on Tercet human venality flourishes, thought Tyrees. The killer he hunted—or thought was hunting *him*—was not only long dead, but also the victim of cruel persecution. "Uni-shad . . . I've been haunted by a ghost," he muttered.

"What did you say?"

He looked at those eyes, full with pain and defiance, and he remembered their lovemaking and her washing of his clothes.

"You had an unlucky birth," he said, "and now you're haunted by a ghost. Put it all behind you. You are young. Look ahead."

Her face softened. She reached out to touch his cheek with her fingertips. "I will look at *you*," she said.

The place she touched grew hot. "Forget the past."

"You know that isn't possible. Why say it? I *am* my past—as you are yours."

"Did you know Meta-sol?"

"A Seer. I have heard his name."

"He was one, at least, who had sympathy—and admiration for your father. He once told me that his own concept of the black hole was the cycle of the past dictating the future: history as an ugly, dark circle, a trap of our own making."

She tilted her head in thought. "Yes . . . my father would have liked that."

"Then listen to them both."

"I can listen. I can even agree; but I don't think it will change me. . . . If I were a man, and not my father's daughter, I might be a Seer by now. Do you believe that?"

"Yes," he said, without thinking, though he wasn't certain.

She had many of the physical capacities of an adept, but that was not enough. He wanted to retreat into himself, then reach out to her. Only then would he know, but he was still too weak. Perhaps he was also afraid.

"Could I become a Seer among the hidden stars, Radis?"

He told her a second lie—the first being his name. "I don't know, Cubis. The New Covenant is young. They are still feeling their way, and I don't know much about it."

She frowned. "But . . . you said you knew the Seers . . . and Meta-sol. How did you know of his connection with my father?"

Tyrees cursed himself for the slip. He reminded himself that Cubus was not a credulous Tercian field worker, and blamed his carelessness on his weakness and his fascination for this woman. He was tempted to tell her everything, but he did not want to face the deeper issues that would arise.

"My Cadre work—and curiosity—often bring me into contact with Seers," he said. "Many in the Regnum are already devotees of the New Covenant. It has an amazing following—I guess because of the Vitar. Meta-sol and I became friends. I remembered the name—Uni-shad. Meta-sol talked about him once as a . . . well, a 'maverick' he said, but one for whom he had great admiration."

Cubus thought about this, and nodded. "Yes, I remember now too. . . . I was a little girl. A Seer with a wispy beard came to talk to my father . . . several times over several years. We had few other visitors then. Would he be the one?"

"Yes. I think Meta-sol was trying to reconcile your father with the community of Seers."

"That fits," she said with a melancholy look. "He was always disturbed by those visits, but I was happy here on the desert, with my father. I didn't care about anything else."

"But not Uni-shad?"

Tears filled the dark round eyes. "I . . . realize *now* that he felt . . . abandoned, betrayed, perhaps wasted. But after my mother died, he could never go back to them."

Tyrees believed her, but a thought kept nagging at the edges of his consciousness, just as the memory of a deadly, jagged sound in the desert night did. Belief or disbelief was irrelevant to a mind trained in the Cadre, and he had no certain proof that Uni-shad was indeed dead.

"How did your father die? I was under the impression that Seers possess powers of self-healing that—"

"They do. But they are not immortal, Radis." She delivered this impatiently, resting her head in her hands and her elbows on the table, but she answered his question. "He fell into a fever. Common here on Tercet, but not often serious. He *let* it take him."

Light squirmed into the small hut through chinks around the shutters, casting sharp stripes and lurid medallions on the table. Tercet was under the high heat. Tyrees toyed with the irony in his head: a unique man developing unique powers over most of a lifetime—then not using them to save himself. There was something . . . *appropriate* about it all.

"So he didn't resist it."

Cheeks still framed by her hands, Cubus shook her head so violently that her short, dark hair flew back and forth. "No. He *welcomed it.* That's when I began to realize just how much he had been suffering all those years."

"You had no help?"

"He wouldn't permit me to ask for it. He said that my mother had no one, so why should he? He spoke almost nothing else during the week it took him to die." She sniffed, and wiped her eyes, but kept her voice steady. "I buried him myself, out there." She looked at a shuttered window. "Near where I found you. You almost fell on his grave."

Tyrees could think of nothing to say. All the wisdom that could be poured into words—which was not much, he suspected—would mean nothing. He took her hand from her face and held it again—the simple, ageless gesture of countless lovers and those who wished to give comfort. He did not know which he was.

He held her hand in the gloom until she looked up sadly, face wan with the draining of emotions, but somehow content.

"I did not know how . . . good it would feel to talk to someone about my father."

"Then I'm glad it was to me."

"So am I," she said quietly. "I wonder if . . . it *had* to be you."

He shook his head. "I think it was because I'm a stranger—and an outsider. Tercet has become a prison to you."

She frowned, but did not disagree. With the fingertip of her free hand she began to trace the outline of one of the errant bulbs of light on the table.

"We have talked about my secrets, but little of yours. I am no longer a stranger to *you*. You know all that is important to me. Tell me about *your* prison. I know you have one, Radis."

Tyrees opened his mouth to speak, to tell her anything—everything. To tell her of his "prison" whose walls he saw less clearly than the ones around him now. But he could not. There was too much that he did not understand, too much that was alien to her. And the Cadre man was there still. He took her other hand. They sat there in silence for a time, looking at the intimate curl of four hands, ten fingers intertwined.

"I know it's not fair," he said, "but you must understand. It's as I said before. Knowledge of certain things about me can cause harm. It is temporary, though. You will know in time."

"When you take me to the hidden stars?"

"Yes."

"But . . . what if harm comes to *you*? You were almost killed before my eyes! Who is this man you look for?"

"I don't know his identity."

"But he came *here*. Is he Tercian?" Her eyes suddenly grew so large that their dark irises were wholly encased with white. Her fingers tightened on his. *"Is he a Seer?"*

He marveled at her intuition. "I . . . don't know that either, Cubus. He's probably off-planet by now. Please, no more questions."

She threw his hands away roughly. "You are waiting to see whether he will kill you," she screamed.

He grabbed her by the shoulders and pulled her to him. "No,

Cubus. I don't intend that to happen. I'm not alone." He placed his hands on either side of her face and looked into her eyes until they calmed. "Your *father* wished to die. I do not."

She looked down. "I am sorry . . . I do not know if losing the hidden stars . . . or losing *you*, frightened me more."

"I will see to it that you leave here, whether I come to harm or not, Cubus."

"You can do that?"

"I can."

"You must have . . . power in your Cadre."

"I do."

She sighed, and lay her head on his shoulder. "I am tired. I cannot remember ever feeling so . . . tired."

"Rest then. Sleep. I'll be fine."

"You rest with me." He felt her laugh without sound. "Or must I prepare more oil?"

Twenty

THREE DAYS LATER, under the harsh glory of the Tercian sunrise, they stood together looking down at Uni-shad's grave. It was the simplest of resting places—unmounded and unmarked except for the circle of stone. When no one remained to tend to it, and the circle decayed through the actions of wind or animal, there would be nothing except the mark in the night sky of which it was a symbol. This was considered appropriate.

She pointed. "There. That is where I found you."

The spot could have been a grave without the circle of stone, for there was only brightless red sand. He put an arm around her shoulders and pulled her to him.

"I guess it's time."

She nuzzled into his neck. "No. Please. You are not well enough."

"You know I am. I should have left yesterday."

"I know that you do not yet see as well as I."

He chuckled softly. "No . . . and I never will again. The

155

damage is permanent. But I can see well enough, and the light doesn't bother me anymore.''

He loved to watch her wonderful eyes grow full, as they did now. ''Are you certain you can find your way? I can take you back to Luta. . . .''

''I'm certain.''

In fact, though he had lost an acuity of sight that an ordinary man would have found incredible, the passage through his desert purgatory had given him another in return—the only one that all Tercian Seers possessed in common—the ability to ''see'' without eyes. Objects did become two-dimensional and informed by fuzzed lines, and distance was manifested in terms of color brightness, but quantity of light was irrelevant.

She turned her back on the grave and looked up at him. ''I will sleep under your cape at night. It is the most wonderful cloth.''

''Good. I'll like thinking about that.''

Reluctantly he released her and began walking into the sunrise, a small backpack dangling from one hand. He put one foot in front of the other with great deliberateness, not wanting to look back. He counted them. He judged that when he counted to a hundred—perhaps two hundred—she would no longer be visible, and then it would be time to think of things buried more deeply in the sand of his mind than Uni-shad was in the sand of the desert. He was able to count seventy-seven.

''Radis!''

He turned, and saw her there. As he did not want to see her, alone in the desert.

''Come back to me, Radis!''

She stood out sharply in the landscape, hand on hip, legs spread wide, one arm and one finger pointed at him like an accusation. Her cry was not a pleading; it was strong and full of power. A command.

''Do you hear? If I *never* leave this desert, you come back to me! You come back!''

His throat constricted and he could say nothing. He nodded his head; before the second nod was complete, she whirled on her heel and strode away like a proud animal.

He watched her move because he knew she would not look back. When she disappeared behind a knoll, he resumed his own march full of perplexity. He was cowed by the effect she had on him. He had not been able to speak. Not since his adolescent years had raw feelings dictated response. It was a victory of sorts, and it was a loss. Despite the circumstances, his time with Cubus had been spent as an ordinary man. When she walked out of his sight, he was the Vitar again—a very special man with extraordinary powers faced with extraordinary challenges, not all of them external.

He made use of the long trek to become reacquainted with himself. Like a long-injured athlete, he tested untried muscles, both mental and physical, and found them intact . . . until the time came to tap his memory as only a Seer can.

When the sound of sharp edges came . . . when it probed the bubble that was Kreat-mel like a deadly insect with its stinger of poison . . . when he felt it thrust and then pierce . . . he could not stop it! He was next to die! There was an instant of pain at the instant of penetration before he fled, for he *was* Kreat-mel until then.

The memory was almost as devastating as the happening itself; only his awareness of it as a thing of the past kept him from literally repeating the experience. He did not know then, and he did not know now, if he would have lived had he remained within the bubble that was Kreat-mel. He thought not, but that did not make the memory of his flight, the abandonment of his latest "father," easier to accept. Whether in the strength of his powers or of his courage, he had been found wanting.

Simultaneously, in another mode of consciousness, he walked blindly, unerringly over the baked earth, using his costly new sight because it was novel to him and because his eyes were still sensitive to the blazing light.

Why had the murderer spared him? No mental effort was necessary. A knife or a stone would have sufficed as he lay there mindlessly scraping out his own grave in the sand. How far away had the killer been? Did that matter?

To make things worse, he was back to the first question. *Who was he?* From the moment when he had read the passage in Meta-sol's diary, his conviction that Uni-shad was the killer had never ceased growing. All he had learned in the interim—at the cost of how many lives?—was that he was wrong, and that the Vitar, the galaxy's demigod, was a mouse in the paws of a cat.

His steady, mechanical pace devoured the miles as his thoughts devoured his mind. He could not escape the word. *Nemesis.* And he was faceless. A mask. A madman. And there was still another mask—Shaamlik. And the enemies of the New Covenant, and the faith of close friends and distant worshippers he could not face shattering. . . .

He stopped. He opened his eyes and the colored desert swam in the sudden light.

A mask . . . mad . . . Shaamlik.

He swayed in the heat. *Who was responsible for her mask and her madness but he?* Is it possible that *she* . . . ?

No. No. Ridiculous. He had watched her slow wasting on a catatonic's bed for almost three years. She loved him. She had no gift for the Learning. No opportunity to kill. No time . . . Guilt, welcome guilt, washed over him with the desert's hot wind.

But the episode taught him how wild and random his thinking had become. He nudged himself into that layer of his mind closer to sleep which created tranquility, allowed meditation or easy musing, but dampened the flow of electrochemical stimulants to his brain. The passions were dammed. He closed his eyes and resumed walking.

Cubus . . . Pity, gratitude . . . or love? Was he still capable of the last? Did he still wish to *have* that capacity? A few days were not enough for such questions, and he could not spend more until larger ones were answered. Still, thoughts of her were balming, mixed with the taste of sweet water and the touch of rich skin . . . and the warm oils of desire. She washed his clothes and she fed him. She healed. She cared.

He walked on through the day and into the night, retracing with steady steps the delirious ones of a mindless stranger of the near past. Inevitably, they brought him back to another, a terrible, beginning. All along he knew; yet the mode of awareness he traveled in would not accept pointless fears. When he came to the place with another bursting sunrise, its features registered even with his nether sight, and he stopped for the second time, for the second time opened his eyes.

There was the rock, there the gnarled tree. There the bed that carried water for a brief spell of Eden once every few years. Yes, this was the place, but there were no bones glossed with the dried spittle of scavengers, no earth stained a deeper, darker red with blood. There was only, on the flat ground, rendered in the Tercian manner, a small circle of stones.

Tyrees's mind writhed like a snake. Its lashings almost broke him out of the discipline of the Learning. Almost. He drew breath and maintained the mode near sleep. This was . . . disturbing; but *anything* he found here would have been disturbing, and it told him nothing. Kreat-mel was not under those stones; he was alive under the knowing mantle of his son's memory. Amen.

Determined not to let fear rule him again, he resumed his march, chewing some of Cubus's tuber vegetable as he went. Anger was better; it had usually served him well, in fact. He raised a fist to the tri-star.

"Come and get me, you warped son of a bitch!" he screamed. "At least I don't hide!"

It was ridiculous, but he didn't care. He felt better. What could he do but do as he must as well as he could? There were worse things than dying—things like believing in the false gods of someone else's making, as he had in the Cadre. Things like having no one who cared. Like Cubus.

So he came back to Luta a different man. Sobered, perhaps even less optimistic, but with an acceptance of his limitations and a higher number in his ledger of values beside the names of such as Bolla and Radis. They cared too. His own value was less an estimate of history, less even than the measure he took of himself, than it was the estimate of those who cared. When he came, after four days of walking without sleep in the usual sense, to the huge round cistern where he and Kreat-mel had their beginning, he was able to smile at the memory.

His arrival at the Emissary found Pristor outside, gazing at an open horizon with small magnifocals. Tyrees was able to stand behind him unnoticed for a time.

"You must be anticipating something, Emissary."

Pristor started. "You! Holy . . . Well, yes," he chuckled. "I was looking for you, of course." He took Tyrees warmly by one arm and led him into the house. "Needless to say, I'm *very* happy to see you. I've aged ten years since you left, thinking about your little 'request' should you not return. Come, you must be hungry—and tired."

When Tyrees was settled into the same chair he had occupied during their long conversation many nights earlier, and food was ordered, Pristor pressed him for his news. He listened anxiously to the quietly toned, tersely phrased account of the events in the desert. His eyes narrowed and he shook his head with incredulity when he heard of the invisible, insidious attack and the death of Kreat-mel. When Tyrees was finished, he was still shaking his head.

"And I thought your safe return meant *good* news. Tercet's only Seer . . ."

"He will be replaced."

"Good. These people will be devastated. . . . Vitar, I advise you to send an original Seer—a Tercian."

"I will."

"And this . . . this *creature* who murders with his mind— you seem to assume he's already off-planet. Can you be sure of that?"

"No. But it's stronger than an assumption. I sense it."

Pristor accepted this without question. "Well, that's a relief. You're safe for the time being."

"If I thought he was still here, I'd have to have Tercet quarantined in any case, now that I know I'm no match for him. At least you would have been spared that responsibility."

"But he's on the loose again."

"I think so. We assumed he was traveling with commercial or trading vessels. Now I think he probably has his *own*, since Tercet has very little traffic and he seems to get around so easily."

Pristor swore softly. "Is that *possible?* How would he get one? How would he crew it?"

Tyrees drew a breath. "That man," he said, "can make anyone do whatever he wants, Emissary."

Pristor resumed his head shaking. "I can't believe it," he muttered.

"Believe it."

"Then why didn't he kill you, Vitar?"

"I don't know. There was a time when I thought he was *only* after me—that he killed the Seers to challenge me, draw me out."

Pristor thought about this. "There is another possibility."

"Yes?"

"That he's afraid of your powers. More afraid than you are of his."

Tyrees remembered the sound of death in the desert. "That doesn't fit the facts."

"Then what does?"

"That he's *not* after me. Only Seers. Here, Kreat-mel was an easy target."

"You are a Seer, Vitar."

"Perhaps he doesn't see me that way."

"How could he not? You are *the* Seer."

"In that case," said Tyrees reluctantly, "he's playing with me."

Twenty-one

We must all seek out the dark, silent places. They are our weaknesses.

—The Sayings of Meta-sol

WHAT LIGHT THERE was in the room shimmered softly off her mask. It was still perfect, still an appropriate barrier enclosing the madness within. Her body also remained the same—or close to the same. There may have been another, almost imperceptible shading toward waste in the time since he saw her last. When he looked upon Shaamlik, he saw death as a winged scavenger, nibbling at leisure at what was already dying.

"Help me, Shaamlik," he whispered. Then, as if afraid of an answer, he hurried from the room and down the corridor. He paused at the entrance to the balcony room when he heard their voices.

"He's got to be protected, that's all." Bolla.

"How? In spite of himself? Tell me how you protect a god." Radis.

"Come now. He's hard to handle, but he doesn't think he's invulnerable."

"No, of course not, but he's growing more desperate. He

thinks that the Maverick has been maneuvering for a one-on-one showdown and that it's inevitable. He'll do anything right now to make just that happen. I can't stop him—and neither can you, Doctor.''

The voices continued. Tyrees didn't know why he was eavesdropping, because he was already aware of the fears of his friends. The cost of their worry about him—and their added responsibilities—during his absence had been high. He could read it most easily in Bolla's aging body. He had not gained or lost weight, but his bulk sagged more heavily. The folds of fat were deeper, more tremulous. Fatigue, grained into the texture and color of his skin, had become a permanent guest. He saw it in Radis, too, but expressed in more subtle ways, for he was younger and trained to absorb stress. Tyrees told himself that these two must not be allowed to become sacrifices as well. Else nothing meant anything.

He entered the room briskly. ''Thank you for coming, gentlemen. Any news?''

''Nothing,'' said Radis. ''The Seer surveillance network is quiet, as it has been since before your trip to Tercet. He's gone to ground.''

''And our search for a source?'' Since Tyrees's return, Radis had pushed the resources of the Cadre to the limit in hopes of unearthing a clue to the Maverick's spawning. He refused to accept the notion that the man had sprung into being as he was, without leaving traces. He was still concentrating on finding a connection to one of the known Seers.

''Negative. But there are still literally thousands of possibilities to check out, so I'm glad he's gone under. That may allow us the time we need to find something.''

Bolla perked up, his jowls aquiver. ''Possibilities . . . you said 'possibilities,' didn't you, Radis?''

Radis looked at him blankly as the old man grew more animated and fished for his blanket of a handkerchief. ''You've thought of something?''

"Yes. But . . . it appalls me that I didn't earlier!" He mopped at the folds in his neck. "Atrophy of the brain. I suppose that I should start to *expect* these—"

Radis interrupted. "Out with it, Doctor! We'll talk about your senility another time!"

"Humph! Well, Radis, my boy! Such vulgar impatience . . . very well. I want your data—all of it. Each and every minutiae gathered during the entire investigation. I'll feed it to Anavex."

"Anavex? Your infamous program? But that's designed for probabilities—*sociological* probabilities, on a galactic scale!"

Bolla's professorial manner reappeared on cue once more. One pudgy finger shot out at Radis. "What is the difference between probability and *possibility*—your word. Can you tell me?"

"Well . . ."

"A number," said Tyrees quietly.

"Right! At least I have one bright protégé. It is a simple matter of degree, my dear Cadre Proctor—the assignment of a weighting number turns a possibility into a probability. Of course, the reverse is also true."

"Look, Doctor," said Radis, exasperated. "I'll try anything. I'll even put up with your pedantry. But I still don't understand how you can use Anavex to tell us anything about the Maverick."

"It'll take some reprogramming to be sure, but I think it's, ah, 'possible,' if not 'probable.' The thing is designed to make predictions based upon massive social and psychological data, as you know, Radis. Its data base is extremely broad and comprehensive. I'll try to put our Maverick in the hopper as a constant, identifying him with all your information, and I may just come up with something."

"Dr. Bolla, we don't *have* any information on the Maverick."

"Ahh, but we do, my boy. We have the times and places of his killings, his methods, some of his movements. We have the very precise nature of his victims, and much of his own extraordinary nature. The capability of murder *by itself* is a strong psychological identifier. With the data base already present in Anavex, we also have the background sociological matrix in which the murders took place.''

Radis's skepticism remained intact. ''So Anavex will tell us who he is, then?'' he said sarcastically.

Bolla's anger was not wholly feigned. ''Of course not, you bumpkin! Pol, how could you have been so foolish as to put this idiot at the helm of a galactic security system?''

Tyrees smiled inwardly. The two men were utterly devoted to one another—and totally incompatible. ''Tell him, Hans.''

Bolla sighed and rolled his eyes to the heavens. ''Obviously, we will get *probabilities*.''

Radis hesitated, then made an apparent effort to remove the scorn from his voice. ''Such as?''

''Perhaps an indication of the Maverick's point of origin; perhaps of the locale of his next strike; perhaps of his motives. Certainly I will be able to build a clearer profile of his personality—if I am given the time.''

''Go ahead then, Hans, but delegate your other duties,'' said Tyrees.

Bolla nodded, uncharacteristically thumbing his nose at Radis. Radis chuckled.

Tyrees looked at the two soberly for a moment, a look that both caught. It drew all three into silence. He had been standing throughout the conversation while the others sat; now he walked to the balcony window and stared out.

''Here it comes, Radis,'' muttered Bolla, sotto voce.

''Doctor,'' said Tyrees to the window, ''why do you say those things when you know I can hear you?''

''I didn't say anything,'' returned Bolla quickly, smugly. ''Sometimes I think those hyperactive senses of yours are mostly hyperactive imagination, Pol. I *may* have cleared my throat there. Did I say anything, Radis?'' Radis opened his mouth, but wasn't given time to speak. ''I've been saying very little, actually. I thought a meeting had been called, so I've been quietly waiting for somebody to say something important.''

Tyrees turned back to them, secretly pleased with Bolla's attempts to lighten their spirits, and put his hands on his hips.

"Do you behave like this at Council meetings, Doctor?''

"Only when they waste my time.'' Bolla watched the suggestion of a twinkle in Tyrees's eyes—the most he could hope for—die with his last words. He knew immediately why.

"Yes—*time*. Something we don't have.'' He spat out the words. "Another Seer will die soon. He's killing our . . . *hope*. We can't afford a plodding, police investigation—as if this man were an ordinary murderer. He's not just erasing people, he's erasing a *belief*—one that promises to bind this galaxy into a healthy society that will grow in new directions!'' Radis and Bolla shrank inwardly from his anger, because it was so rare and so potent. Tyrees raised a fist. "He's got to be stopped before he destroys the New Covenant!''

He stopped suddenly, looking at his fist as if embarrassed by his outburst. He smiled sheepishly and lowered it. "That's how I see things,'' he resumed quietly. "I think Radis will understand why we have to move boldly now, Hans, but you may not.''

Bolla did not like the direction being taken. "Oh? Why not, pray tell? Why must we 'move boldly' at this juncture? I admit that I'm a novice when it comes to tracking down a criminal, but it seems to me that a *plodding* procedure is precisely the one that usually works. Be patient. Gather detailed information. Tap all available resources—like Anavex. Gradually paint your man into a corner. I suspect that most professionals would agree with me.'' He looked to Radis for support, but found only an anxious expression on the Cadre Proctor's face.

Tyrees looked at him too. "Tell him, Radis.'' Radis puffed up his cheeks, making his hero's jaw into a caricature. "Tell him!''

Radis exhaled noisily. "Very well, Vitar. . . . Serial murders. Intelligent killer. No suspects. No clear motive. No hard evidence . . . You *wait*. You establish a pattern. When the pattern gradually becomes clear and predictable, you move *ahead* of him. Eventually, you catch him because you're *waiting* for him—as he is about to strike again." Radis shrugged. "I'm afraid that's the usual scenario, Doctor."

"In other words—you need *time,*" added Tyrees emphatically. "You need more *victims,* in order to establish the pattern. Soon—after one more killing, perhaps—panic is going to start spreading, and the New Covenant will be in jeopardy from *that,* let alone the loss of yet another Seer. So . . ."

"So." Bolla heaved a great, weary sigh. "Here it comes. . . . Allright, Pol. Let's have it. What is the 'bold action' we are not going to like?"

Tyrees smiled grimly. "Like Radis said, we play out the classic pattern. We move ahead of him and wait for him to come to *us.*"

"But *how,* Vitar?" put in Radis, his handsome face creased with lines of skepticism. "We don't know enough about him."

"Bait."

"Beg pardon?"

"The one thing we know for certain is that he wants Seers dead . . . a shark after minnows. We offer him promise of a *feast.*"

"I think I know where you're headed," said Radis in a very soft voice. "It's too . . . dangerous, Vitar. A security nightmare. And he will know."

"Maybe," said Tyrees. "But he won't be able to resist the bait anyway. He's a *mad* shark. He'll come."

Bolla almost yelled. *"What?"*

Tyrees turned to the window. "A Gathering. For the first time among the hidden stars, I summon a Gathering of the Seers."

Twenty-two

Anticipation. *Anticipation is both the black hole and the tri-star; it is our glory and our misery; it defines us with the shapes and shades of horror and ecstasy. Anticipation is the newly bursting love for a woman, the discovery of a dream, the awakening of possibility. It is also the dark mirror into which we look with despair after hopes are won.*

—Uni-shad

THE GATHERING. NEWS of it ripped through the galaxy like hailstones. Believers and unbelievers, the skeptics and the curious, all took recognition of its significance, for it marked the birth of the new Regnum for good or ill, or it signaled man's latest and most vast, most daring crusade, be it fueled by folly or revelation. The storm allowed anything but dispassion. It was one of those rare phenomena that had the farmer nodding with his wife, the businessman putting aside his wares, the politician voicing his uncertainty to an enemy, the dissolute and wealthy alike breaking out of their closed circles of awareness.

The Gathering. The name itself called for spectacle—and so it had been for a long forgotten time on a long forgotten world. To be sure, spectacle had not been its raison d'être on Tercet when the first Seers gathered a thousand years ago, nor had it been when the Vitar became a Seer less than a decade before this latest was called; nevertheless, such was inevitable when they tested their powers through communal effort. When successful, the results *had* to be spectacular, for things were done that even the technocracy beyond the black hole would deem miraculous.

On Tercet a Gathering was called in a time of crisis for decision making, or regularly at three-year intervals so that individual Seers could share their progress and teach each other. The final exercise of each Gathering was a joining of minds and an attempt to accomplish some feat of communal power. The last successful attempt—made possible when, after four generations of failure to bring it about, Tyrees joined the Gathering—they were able to set a huge pyre of wood ablaze. From that time on the Seers, men who had always been venerated like living saints, venerated *him*.

"It was *you,* Pol of the hidden stars," Meta-sol had said. "It was your power, your guidance. . . . You—are—first—among—us." That marked the beginning of the New Covenant—and the coming of the Vitar. This present date, SY 3057, would mark the first Gathering on a galactic scale. Although Tyrees was using it to draw out the Maverick, he was serious about its traditional functions as well, and prepared accordingly.

The setting, as it had been on Tercet, was a natural one open to the sky in the foothills of one of Regnum's mountain chains, for the original desert Seers had always espoused high places. Though the area was relatively isolated, no attempt was made to restrict visitors except in the actual meeting place—a bowl scoured out of the foothills by glacial action many millions of years earlier.

The arrivals of the Seers from the distant star systems took several weeks; each was covered by the various media voraciously. Their appetite was less centered upon the Seers themselves than upon the growing throngs of onlookers. These included the devout, the curious, and the wrathful. Though no major incidents were reported, scufflings and shouting matches broke out between the first and last groups. The dissidents were followers of the old guard who considered the Vitar a tyrant and feared the coming of a galactic theocracy ruled according to the whims of religious fanaticism. The believers—some of them were indeed fanatics—scorned their antagonists with equal fervor.

Since the ascension of the Vitar, the New Covenant had risen far beyond the status of a cult. It grew in its host body like living fire, but no one could say if it would become truly, benignly symbiotic or unutterably destructive.

The Seers were housed in the Citadel until the time of the Gathering. There, no one was permitted access to them. Though Tyrees had little faith in this, or any other measure of security where the Maverick was concerned, he went along with most of Radis's arrangements; but they were at loggerheads about the Gathering itself.

"Vitar! You do not allow me to perform my function!"

They were in the balcony room. Tyrees appeared almost as gaunt and listless as he had during his time travel forays. New furrows, the indelible etches of some chisel of the mind, had formed high on his skull, encroaching on the pale, stretched skin where hair had once been. He sat slouched into a chair, fingers twisting a thin, copper-colored band on his finger. He spoke calmly, without inflection, in the manner that none but a few had ever known him to alter.

"You perform your function superbly well, Radis—better than I perform mine—but you refuse to accept a condition we *all* share."

He twisted the ring slowly, his eyes now on it rather than Radis, and he did not continue. At first Radis sighed impatiently, but after a moment smiled and nodded to himself, having recognized the mannerism as a part of Meta-sol's legacy, the legacy of the master teacher. The pause for the listener's prompt focused attention, signaled special significance, demanded a greater level of objectivity.

"And that condition?"

"None of us has control over all of the forces that impinge on what we want to do, Radis. *None* of us . . . It would be nice, wouldn't it? To know without doubt that our successes—and failures—were accurate measures of our worth?"

Radis's smile went grim. "I'm not sure it would, Vitar."

"For *me*, it would." Tyrees's voice did not change in volume, but its sounds began to take on sharper edges, as steel is drawn over a stone. "I would prefer to *know*, you see."

Radis lifted one eyebrow. "Perhaps we know too much already. We are a strange species. Knowing can . . . inhibit us."

Tyrees drew his head up from the ring to look at his Cadre Proctor with mild surprise. In spite of his commitment to the Learning, Radis was not given to fine, philosophical speculation.

"I was not referring to our species," he said. "I was referring to *me*." Then he laughed. "Our ship's name is *Condor*. An ancient bird of prey. I can only imagine what it looked like. Deadly, I suppose . . . but think of our bird diving for a rat in the desert. As he is about to strike, the rat sees his shadow for a fleeting second in the sand and bolts for a hole. The condor has only himself to blame. Don't let hunger make you overly eager. Come out of the sun.

"But what if a gust of wind pushes his claws a hair past the mark? He doesn't know if he's starving because he's a lousy hunter or a victim of circumstance or bad luck."

Radis was becoming impatient again. "I take your point, Vitar, but what has it got to do with security for the Gathering? Aside from other considerations, your safety is essential for the smooth growth of the New Covenant. That's the simple reason I want the whole area cleared, and not just the cite itself. You won't let me do my job. *You won't let me come out of the sun!*"

"Then any failure is mine, not yours, Radis," said Tyrees mildly as he slowly twisted the ring. Radis noticed it for the first time. It was a plain and unobtrusive band, the kind a child of a poor family would wear.

"But why *invite* disaster? Why have any security at all?"

Tyrees sighed. "Because the measures you have taken will be sufficient to stop anyone *but* the Maverick. That is what I want."

"Then you *have* what you want," said Radis angrily. "All

the preparations have been made for sunset tomorrow.'' He whirled and strode for the exit, fists clenched at his sides.

"Radis."

The Cadre Proctor stopped, but only his head turned. A pinched expression, the look that traps pain and fear, was locked uncharacteristically into the bold, handsome features.

"It's the only way, Radis. He won't surprise me this time. And I'll have my Seers."

Radis opened his mouth to speak, then clamped it shut. He nodded curtly and left.

Twenty-three

There is a moment in time, a moment of decision that each man must face alone. If he fails to recognize the moment, if he fails to decide, then he is like most of us—not truly a man; he has failed to mine the rich lode deep within his soul that once lifted him out of the primeval muck.

—The Sayings of Meta-sol

THE BOWL HIGH in the mountains was one of nature's capricious, teasing gestures to the artist, for the artist reforms, however subtly, the stuff of nature's raw chaos into a suggestion of order and understanding. She knows beauty; indeed, she is beauty itself, and man cannot add to it; but her manifestations of order are rare. As if to deny man any sense of dominion, she occasionally offers such a setting. This was one. The bowl was molded with a particularly exact artist's precision between the sloping shoulders of three high foothills beneath a towering mountain. It was round and symmetrical. Colors of sky and leaf and rock blended perfectly. The late afternoon air remained soft and cool.

From high above, what appeared to be yet another astonishing manifestation of natural order—row upon row of white dots circling the inside of the bowl—was really the defiant stamp of man's own demand for symmetry: the Seers. Shawled and bearing their canes, they sat with nature's stillness, nature's silence, awaiting the setting of the sun. Each waited in his own dark world, for each was blind, but all felt a communion here—and a power—that no ordinary, sighted man would ever feel.

A thousand meters below them, and several times that in distance, an uncounted multitude was massed on the plain. It waited, too, though with little tranquility; it seethed restlessly like a giant amoeba. All the many factions that had any interest—pro or con—in the New Covenant were represented there. The media, especially hungry now, were there. Hundreds of military personnel were there. Black rocks of stern passivity in this anxious flow of humanity, the Cadre was there.

The three men stood in the shadow of a small air car a minute's climb from the rim of the bowl. Radis was grim-faced but silent, standing a few paces away from the other two and staring darkly at the multitude below. Tyrees had the demeanor of a man utterly at peace with himself and his world—relaxed and calm, smiling gently, the intensity of his blue eyes unusually softened. It was an aspect that the other two had learned was totally deceptive. Bolla was visibly agitated, for he was still pressing an argument that was now several hours old.

"I *know* that conclusions at this stage have to be suspect, Pol. Anavex's new programming is far from complete. I *admit* that. But her preliminary findings simply cannot be ignored!"

"They are not 'findings,' Hans. Only probabilities—probabilities arising out of incomplete programming and insufficient data."

"Granted." Bolla drew out his gargantuan handkerchief and rolled it between his palms. "Nevertheless, the figures are so overwhelming! I tell you again—two outrageously high probabilities: 91.4 percent—*91.4*—the Maverick's source-ground is Tercet! And 67.7—the motive is revenge!"

Tyrees remained unperturbed. "Assuming these figures are valid," he said, "and by your own admission they are not, there is nothing to act upon."

"But there is!" Bolla flung the large ball of his handkerchief to the ground and pointed at the bowl's rim above them. Their shadows were now elongated, stretching up the steep slope toward it. "Most of those Seers are Tercians! *The Maverick could be any one of them.*"

"No, Doctor." Radis had turned from his vigil to speak for the first time. "All the Seers have been thoroughly checked out. Not one of them has had the time or the opportunity for all of the killings. If he's anywhere, he's down there." He kicked at loose shale, sending it in a small cascade down toward the mob on the plain.

Tyrees's smile broadened. "Even if one of you were right, I'd still go ahead with the Gathering. It's the only way." He looked over Radis's shoulder at the dying sun. Its last light was simmering just above the plain's horizon. "I thank you both . . . for caring."

With that he turned and began his climb up the slope. He had to lean into it because of the steepness, and from time to time one hand would touch the earth. As the light faded behind them, Bolla and Radis watched his figure moving upward.

Bolla's words were a whispered prayer. "We should have stopped him."

"How?"

Radis waited until he saw Tyrees etched by the last rays of sunlight against the darkening sky at the bowl's rim. Then he ran to the air car and pulled from beneath a seat a powerful lasgun. His eyes were wild as he passed Bolla and headed up the slope on the run.

"There's a radio link from below," he shouted. "If there's a question, tell them to kill."

Bolla stared with mouth agape. Radis tore up the slope silently, but with the impossible, frenzied speed of a madman. He was almost halfway up when Tyrees's diminished form was swallowed by the high, burning mouth of the rim as he descended into the bowl.

Without sound, the Seers stirred. They sensed the sudden presence of their Vitar among them like a school of fish feels a change in the current of a river. As he came down through them toward the bowl's center, the tender filament of communal awareness they had been holding expanded, took on strength. By the time he had passed the last circle of silent Seers and stood alone at the bowl's nexus, their filament had metamorphosed from dull gossamer to shining glasteel. The Tercians among them had felt this once before many years ago, but this was even stronger, so they rejoiced anew. The new Seers were so awed that they lost concentration for a time, and the net of wondrous awareness faltered in places until they felt a guiding touch bring them back to add their power to the net. It was the touch of their Vitar, their Life-Giver, and it inspired them to stretch to the limits of their strength.

There was a time of adjustment, for every Seer was conscious of two awarenesses interfacing—that of his self and that of the net—and each had to struggle delicately, shifting in the eye of his mind for the perfect mesh of his giving and the net's receiving. When that state was achieved, the awareness of self was a dim, distant shadow. The communion was complete. The net was glorious. In their unity, they felt omnipotent. The shadows of their selves exulted as they waited for direction from their Vitar.

No words were spoken—none had been since they entered the bowl—but the wishes of their Vitar were communicated nevertheless through the filaments of the net. One thought. If the thought were voiced, it would be cradled in one word.

Light.

Some of the hearts within the distant shadows quailed momentarily, but the merest touch from the Vitar renewed their courage.

Light.

The edges of the net began to pull into its center, very slowly, and the Seers felt/saw the pull as palpably as stretched skin. They understood immediately what was to be done. They summoned full concentration and channeled their forces to the radial pulling in begun by the Vitar. It was like the action of a snake tightening into a coil, only this was slower and infinitely more intricate. As the snake feels itself tightening inward, so did they—and light began to build.

The net in the most basic terms was a form of controlled energy. Now, like a collapsing star, the dispersed energy was being forced into greater and greater concentration. The Seers and their Vitar were squeezing light out of themselves.

Radis, as he crouched low at the top of the bowl's rim, his grip on the lasgun hard and ready for he knew not what, was the first to see it. Only a dull green glow at first, it seemed to emanate from the bare ground at Tyrees's feet. He wiped his eyes and blinked. It was there, faint and pulsing slowly. He knew this must be part of the ceremony of the Gathering, but Tyrees, standing alone in the center with head down and shoulders bowed, and the rows of white-shawled Seers around and above him, were as still as death.

The green light grew stronger. Radis had difficulty now picking even the dark figure of Tyrees out of the brightness of its center. The rhythm of its pulse grew as well. Afraid and amazed, he watched it climb up the walls of the bowl through the Seers. Like no other light he had ever seen, it seemed to have a defined boundary, a distinct limit that was expanding with each pulse. As it passed each white row, the seated forms were obliterated. Green . . . so green . . . bright and rising . . . bright to the verge of pain.

Pain!

Convulsively, Radis rolled away from the rim and down the slope. Stars were still exploding on the backs of his eyes when he pulled himself behind a boulder to rub them. In a few moments he was able to squint back up the slope. The green light was overflowing the rim like the magma of a volcano— except that it was flowing upward into the darkening sky. He flung the lasgun to the ground.

From the plain below a dim glow was visible even before the light had escaped the bowl and a thousand fingers pointed.

"Look!"

"Up there! Below the mountain! Look!"

"See the light? It's getting brighter!"

"It's green! It's . . . That's where the Seers are!"

"Ohmygod! . . . *Ohmygod!*"

"What are they doing? Can they be doing this?"

"What's happening? . . . What's *happening?*"

"The whole mountain's on fire!"

As the green globe of light rose and expanded, so did the sounds from the plain, sounds that plumbed every range of human emotion. Prayers mixed with curses, wails discorded with cheers, screams clashed with cries of exultation. Their mingled sounds became a roar that grew as the light grew. Some shook fists, some fell to their knees, some simply stared and cried tears of wonder.

As the light grew more and more intense, the roar became more fluted with sounds of fear. Thin shrieks. Gasps. A green sun hung above the mountain and washed the plain with merciless light, washed the faces of the multitude with such fierce scouring that some began to fall upon the ground, covering their eyes and fearing retribution for their sins. Some began to run.

Tyrees was bursting with it. He was their Vitar. He was their center of light. He was also near exhaustion, and he sensed that of the Seers; yet he had taken them this high, higher than any man had ever climbed, and he wanted to revel in it. He had not intended to drain himself like this, but now he found that he wanted all to know. He wanted all to *know*.

Finally, with the last of his strength ebbing like a tide, he began to let slip the fist of his control on the net's now tight constriction. The green fury of light high above the mountain had already begun to fall when the sound came.

It came out of the desert from a hundred light-years away. It came from a place of suffering behind a black hole and buried in the dark recesses of his soul. The sound of ragged edges. The jagged, cutting sound that had ripped through him to destroy yet another father.

He reached desperately for strength that was already spent.

Like fine grains of sand through his fingers, he felt the net slipping out of his control. He panicked. The hideous sound was overwhelming, invading the net, invading all but the pale shadow he had left quivering behind. He fled to it.

He found himself sitting in the center of the bowl, tottering loosely like a newly born, soft-boned infant. The light was surrealistically bright. Bright and green. Through pinched eyes he looked about him. The Seers ranked around and above were as still as before, as silent as before. But all of them wore expressions of horrible agony.

He screamed.

He plunged madly back into the net. It was contracting again, now a snake writhing convulsively into a closed coil of pain, a throat closing against its own source of life. His shadow screamed again. He fought against the constriction deliriously, a wrestler struggling with insane will when strength was gone. For a time he succeeded in pushing apart the coils. Then the sound found him again.

It screeched into him like a banshee, but this time he would not let go of his hold on the net. The screech intensified to a point where he felt himself being torn apart by it. But he didn't care anymore. He screamed once more. ''Kill me then!'' And he waited, twisting still against the hellish sound, to die.

Then, in the place where his shadow kept yet a tenuous existence, he felt an impact, and all was blackness.

When Radis heard the Vitar's first scream, he didn't consider options. He reacted under the impulse of pure instinct. This was his leader. This was the man who had saved his life. He scrambled from behind his boulder and lurched back up the slope with a forearm flung across his eyes. By squinting downward, he was able to see the ground in front of his feet well enough to make the rim quickly. That was when he heard the second scream, and the light was growing even brighter . . . but he had to see! Forcing his eyes open against the glare, he plunged down into the bowl through the motionless Seers, careening against several of them. At the bottom, through tearing, burning eyes, he saw Tyrees writhing like an epileptic on the ground.

"Kill me then!"

Radis stood there, breathing heavily, not knowing what to do. The pain in his eyes was eroding his will to keep them open. Finally instinct took over again, and he took the one step that placed him over Tyrees's convulsing body and hit him in the face with his fist as hard as he could.

The body grew still. As Radis was kneeling to it, the light flared higher again, this time to an impossible intensity, before falling finally into the blackness of the night.

Twenty-four

You will come to know . . . that there is more to be purged than sight. . . . Remember, Pol of the hidden stars, life itself is a purging.

                           —The Sayings of Meta-sol

"THE DETAILS. GIVE me the exact details."

Bolla sighed. He looked at Tyrees carefully again, and could see no sign of physical damage except deep fatigue; it had been two days since the Gathering, and Tyrees had returned from some state between sleep and coma only a few hours ago.

"Very well. Over four hundred were injured when the crowd panicked—twelve fatally. Several dozen suffered eye damage, but only two will be permanently blind."

"Like Radis."

"Yes. . . . Pol, you need rest. This isn't necessary. Why wallow in it?"

Tyrees ignored the comment. "How many Seers?" he asked.

Bolla had remained standing throughout their talk, something he never did by choice. Now he heaved his bulk with resignation into the large armchair always reserved for his use when he came to the top floor of the citadel. Though fatigue had etched fine, telltale lines into the face of Tyrees, his was devastated by it. Gray, blotched skin, hanging, slack-fleshed jowls, heavy bluish pouches under the eyes had turned a face perfectly befitting a jolly old man into unwholesome decay.

He glanced at a printout. "Sixteen dead. Four others are still alive, but they may not recover."

Tyrees nodded. "The toll mounts." He spoke matter-of-factly. "No sign of the Maverick, of course."

"None."

"We can't even rule out the Seers?"

"Not really, though none of them came out of the Gathering in good shape. . . . Pol, they're asking about you. They want to see you. They're . . . afraid, I guess, and very concerned about you. So is everyone else out there." Bolla gestured to the balcony window.

"Not everyone, Doctor. This mess will really bring out the wolves . . . and I don't blame them."

"Pol—"

"I'm quitting, Hans." The blue eyes looked directly at Bolla for the first time. They were weary, washed, dull, defeated.

Bolla shook his head angrily. "No, Pol. You can't do that. Too many people—"

"Too many people have become *sacrifices* . . . to their god."

Bolla heaved himself out of the chair. His jowls shook and his voice was cracking. "A noble gesture like that one, Pol Tyrees, will plunge this whole damned galaxy into chaos!"

"We're not far from that now."

"Don't be—"

"It's not nobility, Hans." The soft light gleamed off Tyrees's skull as he shook it back and forth. "I'm sick of it all."

Bolla crumbled back into the chair, sputtering. "So you're just going to hand us over to the Maverick? You're going to let us become his play dolls?"

"I can't stop him."

"You can damn well try!"

Tyrees looked at him strangely. But Bolla was a psychologist and had made this man his study for many years, so he was able to read the look. It said, "I have tried to the depths of my soul, and I have been found wanting." The professional in Bolla overcame the man, cautioned him not to press further. Time. Play for time. He brought out his handkerchief and struggled for calm.

"What will you do, Pol?"

Tyrees shrugged his indifference. "Tell the Seers to select another Vitar, I suppose. It may be that the people won't want another."

"No. I mean, what will you do with *yourself?*"

Tyrees fingered his ring. It was the only suggestion of adornment Bolla had ever seen on his person—and he could not remember seeing this one before.

"I don't know. . . . Perhaps I'll go back to Tercet for good. Maybe I'll just . . . travel."

"And the Maverick? Is he going to leave you alone?"

"Who knows?" The tone said, *Who cares?* "You did say his motive was revenge. . . . If I quit, maybe he'll have it. Maybe he already has it."

"And Shaamlik?"

Tyrees rose abruptly. "Yes. It's past time for my visit. Thank you for coming, Hans." He walked slowly to the mouth of the corridor that led to Shaamlik's room and turned there. When he spoke, there was real concern in his voice. "Look after yourself, Hans. You need rest."

Bolla smiled back at him from his chair. He waved his handkerchief like a flag of surrender. "I was just about to say the same thing to you, my boy. . . . Will you do me one favor?"

"Of course."

"Give it a few days? Get some rest yourself and decide nothing for a few days? . . . Please, grant an old man one last indulgence."

Tyrees hesitated, frowning. Then he nodded and left the room. Bolla stared at the spot where he had stood.

"Holy . . . jumping . . . shit," muttered the old man to himself.

As always, Shaamlik's mask was unchanged. Fingering the light coverlet as he moved softly around the bed, Tyrees took some solace in that. She was always the same. She was always here. Her breathing was so light and shallow that it was almost imperceptible. But she was here, and he could remember with painful exactness how the face behind the mask was supposed to look. The tawny hair, the fine nose, the lift in one corner of the full mouth when she was secretly pleased. When he was with her here, she always brought him back to a better time—a hard time, but one still of hope.

His head came up abruptly when he heard the scraping sounds. No one ever presumed to interrupt him when he was with her. There was a whole team of medics with Shaamlik's care as their sole responsibility, but he almost never saw them. They monitored her status from another room and avoided the Vitar when they could, as he did them—for they embodied an ugly truth.

He listened. When he heard the shuffling sounds underlying the scraping, he knew. "Not now," he whispered, but he moved to open the door.

Radis, with an intense look of concentration stamped on his lowered face, had already gone down the passage past the entrance. A cane—a Seer's cane—halted in its tracing of the juncture of floor and wall on the other side of the corridor. He was stooped awkwardly because the cane was too short. A medical band passed over his eyes and around his head. He straightened at the hiss of the opening door and smiled.

"Vitar? Is that you, Vitar?"

Tyrees could not speak.

"Of course it is! Who else would be there? Damnit, I'm on the wrong side of the corridor, aren't I?"

Radis was an absurd figure. A superbly-muscled athlete's

body; strong, handsome facial features that belonged on a statue; the caped Cadre uniform with the solid black collar piping that could only be worn by one man holding the highest security office in the galaxy—all carried by a man with the aspect of an infant just escaping from his crib.

"Hello, Radis."

"There you are. Couldn't find you in the balcony room. Sorry to come when you're visiting with Shaamlik, but I didn't know. And I don't like them leading me around."

"How are you?" The question was inane, but Tyrees was only trying to fill silence.

Radis laughed. A real laugh. Tentatively, he stretched one arm out to touch the near wall and gathered in his cane. "I'm just fine! How are *you?*"

Tyrees squeezed out an answer. "I'm fine too." He reached to take Radis's hand from the wall. "Come and sit down." He led Radis like a child into Shaamlik's room and helped him sit on a small stool, the only piece of furniture there excepting the bed. They had trouble with the cape. When he was settled, Tyrees looked from him to Shaamlik and back.

"I hear you saved my life."

Radis beamed. "I hope so. I sincerely hope so. You saved *mine.*"

Tears formed in Tyrees's eyes. He could allow this, knowing they could not be seen. But his voice was steady. "I managed to do it and stay intact."

"Yeah . . . but I'm clumsier," chuckled Radis.

"I'm sorry, Radis."

Instantly, Radis turned serious. "I'm not. You're alive. Maybe you would have come through without me, but I'd like to think not."

"I . . . you're right. I would have joined the sixteen Seers."

Radis tapped his cane lightly on the floor. "This belonged to one of them. He must have been a little fellow. . . . I feel guilty about asking for this thing, but it makes me feel like one of them. . . . I've decided, Vitar."

"Decided?"

"Yes." Radis placed both hands atop the cane and leaned forward, head slightly tilted to one side—a pose very suggestive of Meta-sol. "Believe it or not, I'm glad this happened. The blindness will help me, I know it will. I'm going to enter the apprenticeship, Vitar. I'm going to be a Seer."

Tyrees looked at the blind man and shook his head, now having to fight hard to control his voice. "You're starting rather late."

"I know. But I've already progressed more than you think, and now I'll be able to devote my full time to it. You can't keep me with the Cadre now." He chuckled again. "I have the perfect excuse."

"You could still run the Cadre, Radis, even blind."

"Maybe, but not as well. Please, Vitar, let me use my excuse. . . . Of course, I'll stay on until we nab the Maverick." When Tyrees didn't respond, he continued. "We'll get him this time. He's on-planet and Regnum's closed down tighter than a wine barrel. We'll get him."

He has changed, thought Tyrees. Those trained by the Cadre possessed an inordinately high physical confidence—Radis more than most. That, of course, was gone. But gone, too, was his hard, practical realism, an attitude Tyrees now realized was an adjunct of his duties, not his character. Perhaps blindness *had* set him free, for he now had the naive enthusiasm of a young boy. Suddenly, Tyrees envied him. He envied the man's idealistic lust for the future . . . and his courage. He felt a tinge of shame about his own decision.

"Dr. Bolla told me," he said. "You closed Regnum down *before* the Gathering. That's a pretty big move—not to question its legality—for a Cadre Proctor to make unilaterally."

Radis laughed again. He had laughed with more real humor in the last few minutes—in his blindness—than he had in months. "That *was* presumptuous of me, wasn't it? Well, you can always fire me."

"You knew I wouldn't agree."

"That's right. You *wanted* the Maverick on Regnum and would have been afraid of closing him out. I was only concerned for your safety—so I would have been more satisfied if he hadn't already made landfall before I sent out the order. Obviously, he had—but now we've got him.''

"Or he's got us.''

"Nuts . . . Sorry, Vitar, but I don't buy that. I know he must be an extraordinary man, but he's still *human*. And he's alone. We have the manpower and the resources, and we have him pinpointed—finally—on a single planet. And we have *you*.''

Tyrees winced. We have you. The Maverick's plaything, he thought. Me and the entire body of Seers—now much diminished. The New Covenant seemed as significant now as a child's dream.

"I hope you have the time, Radis.'' (He couldn't bring himself to say "we.'') "Regnum is the seat of galactic government. Her isolation won't be tolerated for very long.''

"Well, maybe the sabotage of the Gathering will actually work in our favor there. The people know about him now, and what he did to us.''

"The New Covenant people, perhaps. What about the others? Do they even *believe* it?''

For the first time Radis was uncertain. He frowned. "I don't know. It's too soon. They're still in shock, I think.''

Tyrees wanted to tell him not to put his faith in people—in people at large, or even in his heroes . . . especially not in his Vitar. They were all too venal. They were all too weak. But he couldn't do that. Not now. Not to him.

"Carry on, then . . . do what you can.''

Radis's head jerked slightly in surprise and he touched the medical band around his eyes with a fluttering gesture. He had expected a long session, a discussion of options and strategies, but there was no mistaking the dismissal. Gingerly, he rose from the stool.

"Ah . . . I will.'' He extended the cane to find the door opening. "Say hello to Shaamlik for me.''

Tyrees listened to the scraping sounds again as they receded down the corridor. He pulled the stool under him and sat for a long time in the semidarkness, watching Shaamlik. He thought about his lost fathers, his lost dreams. He thought about how ridiculously potent he had felt when he was causing a sun to burn over a mountain. The acid of bitterness welled in his mouth. Abruptly he rose.

He spoke softly to Shaamlik. "Let's see if I can use these godlike powers to some *purpose*."

Swinging the head of the surgical bed clear of the wall, he began to position himself, and hesitated. Then he moved to a speaker on the wall and flicked on its switch.

"Medical unit . . . this is the Vitar. You are dismissed until tomorrow morning. Both of you. Acknowledge." At first only startled exclamations came from the speaker. "Acknowledge!"

"Yes, Vitar. Acknowledged."

He returned to stand directly behind and above Shaamlik's head. To his touch the mask was firmer than skin, but still surprisingly warm and resilient. His fingers probed for the interface between skin and mask where the back of her skull met her spine. He closed his eyes, took a deep breath, and the stress lines of his face melted away until his mask was almost as perfect as Shaamlik's. Given their stillness and the nakedness of their scalps, they now looked eerily alike—a king and queen of ancient and alien times, perhaps, rendered immortal by the secret skills of a master embalmer.

Tyrees let himself float slowly down the river of his blood, down into the capillaries of his fingertips, until he could "see" the shadowy wall that resisted the pressure of his passage. On electrical charges of infinitely small power, of infinitely large frequency, he pushed through—first his own skin, then Shaamlik's.

He paused then, for a change of mode was necessary. It involved contact—contact and a mingling on the molecular level. This was intimacy at its most elemental, but it was intimacy without sharing, without soul—and it was dangerous in the extreme, even were this not a mingling with madness. Seers who possessed the capacity to go this far knew that such contact could cause an irreversible change in their own awareness, as much as a sledgehammer impacting on a skull.

Tyrees went carefully, making the contact as gradual, as tentative as possible. He probed and withdrew, probed and withdrew. He was like a radio operator receiving sporadic, truncated messages, each by itself unintelligible; but these messages were not words, or even thoughts. They were images, each with its own powerful, sensual charge. Among the first he "saw" was a single, naked breast; it was accompanied by sensations of warmth, of sucking, of drowsiness. Another was of a male chin from below with drops of perspiration clinging to it; this came with both pain and arousal.

As he probed deeper, Tyrees was increasingly dominated by the power of the sensations. Each time he saw/felt, it was more difficult to identify the source as other than himself. But he would not let himself stop.

Soon the images began to be more unrecognizable, more often attended by pain, and he was able to retreat from them only with tremendous effort. Then he saw the flames. The pain was so intense, the smell so horrifying, that withdrawal was a swift reflex. Tremulous, he hovered. This was the source of the madness. He would have to penetrate it, encapsulate it, control it. He did not think he could . . . but it did not matter. He gathered what strength he still commanded. . . .

And he was jerked roughly back like a naughty boy from a candy counter. His cheek stung from a slap. Dizzy, he opened his eyes. He could not believe them. First he had to speak what they saw.

"Cubus."

Twenty-five

Face the Darkness. Burn thy light into its maw even as it swallows thee. Do this, for ye cannot flee it. Do this, or cower before it.

—The Teraac

HIS RING FINGER tingled oddly. While he stared at her dumbly as if she were an hallucination, he raised it to his chest and clasped it there with his other hand.

Cubus smiled at him warmly. "The ring helps me find you—from horizon to horizon."

Tyrees had to tongue at the inside of his mouth for the moisture to speak. "It's *you*."

She laughed softly, a wonderful sound. Her eyes widened into the huge look of innocent wonder that he loved most. "Of course it's me . . . you should have known."

"You're the Maverick."

"The what? . . . Never mind. At the moment I'm the purser of a trading vessel. See?" Palms outward, she displayed her uniform, one typical of those worn by officers of large merchant ships. It suited the supple body and short, dark hair. "I chose purser because it's a nice, middling rank—even though the ship belongs to me."

Wave after hot, flushing wave coursed through Tyrees. He

was close to being sick with nausea. "You . . . killed . . . Kreat-mel. And all the others."

The smile, and the child's eyes, vanished. "They killed my father."

Now all of it hit him with shuddering impact. A shadow inside struck and left dark bruises on his soul. Uni-shad, the ostracized Seer, the tragic sorcerer . . . the sorcerer's daughter trained in his black magic and touched with madness . . . the jagged sound coming out of the desert . . . even the unholy ecstasy of his lovemaking. Indeed, he should have known.

"You have . . . come here to kill me," he whispered.

The wide eyes returned, along with an expression of genuine pain. "How can you say that? I love you."

"You murdered my Seers. I was trying to find you . . . to destroy you."

"You didn't know who—or why. Now you know." Her voice turned into a hiss. "They deserved to die."

"They did not. And you are not their judge."

"I am. No one has a better *right*—" She bit off her anger and said pleadingly, "But it doesn't matter. Don't you understand? I don't blame *you* for anything."

Tyrees shook his head incredulously. How did the desert— and one man—produce *this*. His stomach turned when he thought of himself entwined with her. He could almost smell the oil.

"Why are you here, Cubus?"

"I've already told you. I love you. You're the only man I've ever met who wasn't weak. I want to stay with you." She took a step forward, but stopped when he moved back. "I wouldn't harm *you*. I don't even know if I *can*. . . . I've always been able to catch you by surprise, you know. But when you begin to struggle—"

"You've harmed me, allright. And you played me like a harp on Tercet."

"I deceived you?" She shook her head and pouted. "I told you no lies. Everything I told you was true." She was speaking in a breathless rush, like a little girl in a hurry to set things right. "There were things I did not tell you, but no lies. I told you about my father and who I was. *You* told me your name was Radis. . . . It's hard for me not to call you that now. . . . I will call you anything you like—except Vitar."

"Call me a fool," he said, overwhelmed by her savage innocence and by the suffering he'd caused in not recognizing it.

She stamped her foot in frustration. "Why do you reject me? We *belong* together. We're not like *them.*"

"Them," he assumed, meant everyone. "The killings, Cubus."

"But you *know* about my father," she cried, curling her fingers into fists in a spasm of anger. Then she sighed and hung her head petulantly. "All right, then. If it will please you, you can have your Seers. I understand. They make you a god. Take them. They are like stupid children anyway . . . and enough have paid. I will be happy now . . . with you."

Tyrees's mind reeled. She displayed no guilt, no sense of the horrible magnitude of her actions—or of his revulsion. "Cubus. You have bloodied a whole galaxy . . . the Gathering . . . all those lives . . . the New Covenant. . . ."

"Pahh!" she spat. "That is folly. Ridiculousness. You simply retard the growth of evolution."

"What?"

"Retard the growth of evolution. My father's words. That is another of the reasons he broke with the Seers. They wanted to turn away from their own growth to teach the people. A waste of time."

Mouth open, Tyrees could only ask, "Why?"

"Can you teach a snake to fly? No. You can only point its eyes at the sky. You teach nothing but a vision of the unattainable. You teach yearning, dissatisfaction."

"Uni-shad's words again."

"Yes."

"But he taught *you.*"

"*I* am not a snake! . . . nor are you . . . my love. I will call you that, until you give me another name. My love."

Tyrees covered his face with his hands. "Oh my God."

She was exasperated. "What is *wrong?* You . . . you remind me of my *father* right now. He could get like this too. He could be infuriating! Sometimes I could just . . ."

Her voice trailed away as she turned her back to him. Tyrees's hands slid slowly from his face. "You fought with your father." Something glimmered in his mind. . . . *You're the only man I've ever met who wasn't weak.* "You fought with him often, didn't you? Like we are now?"

Her shoulders squared. "Yes. The last time . . . the last time he . . . was very angry."

"What happened?"

She whirled back upon him. "Nothing! Why are you asking me these questions?"

Tyrees answered with careful indifference. "Never mind, Cubus. I just thought it would help me understand you better, that's all."

"Oh . . . well, maybe it will. . . . He was angry because of a young man—from the village. He was wrong, that's all. He had no right—" Cubus hesitated, then stopped altogether. She sniffed and wiped at her nose with the back of a wrist.

"He didn't want you seeing him?"

"No. He hurt me."

"Who?"

"The young man. We were lovers, but he laughed at me—and at my *father*. He called us desert rats. I warned him, but he did it again. Do you see?"

"You . . . hurt him back," prompted Tyrees.

Cubus smirked. She held up a thumb and forefinger and squeezed delicately. "I did. I didn't even know I could do it then, but I went inside his head and pinched a tiny part of his mind. He couldn't move his tongue anymore. He will never, ever call anyone names again. I made him dumb. Now do you see?"

And it must have begun even before that, thought Tyrees. Fascinated, as a rodent is said to be fascinated by a reptile, he prodded further. "And that made your father angry."

"Yes! He said that I humiliated him. 'To use what I have taught you for that!' he said. I was proud of punishing a stupid, ignorant farmer because he shamed us like the rest of them, and my father was ashamed of *me*."

Though it had hidden in a nether part of him, Tyrees had glimpsed its dark shifting earlier. Now, clearly, he saw it coming.

"He . . . tried to punish you."

Suddenly Cubus brightened. "Yes. You *do* see! The unfairness of it! He came into my *mind*. My own father! He came into my *mind!*" Then she was just as suddenly frowning—furiously, arms clasped tightly across her chest, her head lowered, one foot scraping at the floor. "He said that I had to learn what it was like and . . . he hurt me."

"You killed him. You killed your father."

She smiled sadly. "Now you know. Now you understand, don't you? Everybody hated us. Everybody hurt us. Then my own father was hurting me too . . . and I am stronger than them all."

Now that he knew some of the ingredients in the fetid stew of her mind, he felt even more powerless against it. His own mind was a mire of revulsion and pity, loathing and sorrow. He knew he should try to lead her on—and kill her if he could. He mustered the words, but they sounded false even to his own ears.

"I understand now, Cubus. You were only striking back. You were scorned and made to suffer by your lessers. You were alone and you found me in the desert, but I was hunting you. . . ."

Her eyes became enormous. "Yes! Yes! I knew I could make you understand, my love."

"Call me Pol," he said as tenderly as he could. "My name is Pol Tyrees."

"Pol . . ." she whispered breathlessly. "Oh, Pol, think of it!

The hidden stars are ours! The galaxy! Together, we can eat it like an apple!''

''Yes . . . if that's what you want, Cubus.''

''It *is* what I want. I want them to *know* me, know what I can do! I am not a rat in the desert—I am *me!*''

With a shock Tyrees remembered his own sentiments when he was creating the green sun. They were the same.

''But right now,'' she said, her voice husky, ''I want you.''

It was yet another abrupt shift. She was like an actress running through a familiar repertoire of roles, each finely honed, cleaving to a different mood or passion—but she was not acting. Smiling slyly, she plucked from a pocket a small vial and unstopped it.

''Look what I brought for us.''

In only a few seconds its odor permeated the room—the heady, lust-laden scent that had returned to his mind, bidden and unbidden, so many times since he had left Tercet. Immediately he was aroused; immediately he was incredulously ashamed.

She set the vial on the stool and provocatively unbuttoned the short uniform jacket. In her he now saw these gestures of seduction as grotesque—yet he wanted her, wanted *only* her. By the time she dropped the jacket on the floor, her nipples were already rigid. Slowly, she picked up the vial, and looking at him with half-lowered eyelids, tipped it delicately, stopping its top with her little finger. After replacing it on the stool, she stepped toward him, the finger coiled and raised to his lips.

He wanted to resist, but he could not. He opened his mouth and she touched the tip of his tongue with her finger. Then came the strong, memory-fed taste of spices and desire, and he was a tight fist, a sealed drum of unburst lust. Its power was such that it alone caused him to hesitate, to wonder. *How can I respond to her like this? She is a murderer of fathers!* How much is the oil? How much *her?* Do I find destruction so alluring? Even as he thought this, he was reaching for her—but she stayed his hand on her breast.

Cubus was looking at the bed—and the form upon it. When her dark eyes turned back to him, something cunning had triggered in them.

"Who is she?"

He licked his lips. "Shaamlik."

"You were trying to help her when I came. Why?"

"She . . . was my friend."

Her eyes flared, narrowed. "She is mad—beyond help, dangerous. Yet you were trying. Why?"

He could feel her breast rise with her suspicion under his hand. Incredibly, horribly, his desire remained. "She helped me in the past."

Cubus brushed his hand aside and moved quickly to the bed. "She will never recover, Pol. She would not *want* to recover with a face like this . . . and we will need this bed." Cubus reached for the tubing that snaked from a closed medical unit to beneath the bed's coverlet.

"No!" he shrieked.

At first she stopped, surprised at the fear in his cry. Then a sneer distorted her features. "So . . . you loved her, did you?" She took a deep breath, calming somewhat. "Very well . . . that is in the past. I will share the galaxy, but I will not share *you*." Viciously she threw aside the coverlet, baring Shaamlik's wasting body.

Rage and desire mingled in Tyrees—and desire died.

"Don't . . . you . . . *touch* . . . her," he growled.

Again she was startled. As realization grew, so did her own rage—he saw it in the flare of nostrils and the cording of neck muscle. He steeled himself. She said nothing, but in an instant her fist was plunging from above her head down toward Shaamlik's exposed neck.

"Huummmph!"

Tyrees's booted foot took her fully in the chest. She crashed against the wall with such force that she slid down it like a flaccid doll, one leg bent under her. A red welt was already forming across her breasts. Breathing heavily—from his emotions rather than his attack—Tyrees lay on the floor opposite her. He could only get to one knee before Cubus opened her eyes. They were full of tears.

"You don't love me at all!" she sobbed. "You're just like my father!"

Still in a fury, he tore the ring from his finger and hurled it at her. She winced as it struck her forehead. A drop of blood gouted there. A moment passed as she blinked in confusion; then another transformation changed her face. She tilted her head to one side and smiled, lips stretched like a gargoyle's over the white teeth. The strange smile, the bare breasts, the unnatural, twisted position on the floor, made her an icon for a demented priest.

"I am going to make you pay," she said.

In the midst of his first step toward her, the jagged sound returned. He retreated into himself, for he could only defend against it there, where it attacked. She had said that she had only taken him by surprise, he thought. Perhaps he could fight. There was nothing else, anyway.

He was a bubble of awareness again, and the sound was a spear of piercing sharpness again—a series of them. He hardened the skin of his bubble and at first managed to repel them, but each one was sharper, stronger than the last. He sensed that her increasing efforts caused her pain also, but his resistance seemed only to lend her more power. It was as if her madness fed upon both her frustration and his fear. Nevertheless he fought with all the hate, all the sorrow, all the despair he could muster. It was only when the bubble that was himself, and the searing edges of sound that assaulted it became indistinguishable, that he gave up.

He abandoned the bubble's skin and retreated even deeper into self. He waited there in the silence once again, to die. He wanted to die. There was no more fear, no more caring. But when the sound found him again, a mechanism took over—one that he did not know existed, for he had assumed that he had long ago taken the audit of all the functions of his mind and body.

Without willing it, without a sense of transition, he was

tossed into the wild current of alien ether to which he had almost become addicted years earlier.

It was time. The flux of time.

There were no beginnings, no endings. A million years was a second, a second a million years. A swimmer in a powerful river can not resist or even influence its flow, but he can ride it downstream. A calm and skillful rider can even touch a bank where he chooses. So it is with time. When a bank is gained, there is only *his* time. It is endless and unshared, but he can watch stars being born—or others of his kind trapped by a second as an insect is trapped by plastic. It is also like a drug of wonderful devastation: under its influence there is awe and ecstasy—but one returns to an ever-quickening death. Ecstasy in large doses is anathema to the human condition. Even as he rode, Tyrees knew this well, and its oblivious fascination was just as tempting now, perhaps more so—but he edged out of the current as soon as he sensed the place. . . .

Cubus was as he expected—half sprawled on the floor, but leaning toward the spot he had occupied a millionth of a millionth of a second before. It was long enough ago, a spate of time lodged in the past like a branch in a narrow stream, for him to do as he wished before time "caught up" with him again.

Cubus's expression still belonged on a gargoyle, but now it was even more feral—and, indeed, because of her stillness, seemed carved from stone. Great strain showed there, strain accompanied by the anticipation of a wolf about to bring down a crippled stag. Only a step or two away, Shaamlik still wore the other mask—this one, though inhuman, more befitted humanity. It made what he had to do easier.

He could do it with a single blow of one hand, but for some reason he shied from that. Instead he picked up the stool by one leg and swung it far back over one shoulder. For the briefest of moments he hesitated. She was utterly defenseless. . . . This was murder. He swore at himself for the absurdity of the thought, and started to bring it down. . . .

And she wasn't there.

"Damn!" Tyrees knew. Not bothering to arrest his swing, he

let the stool fly to shatter against the wall. He dove into the debris and seized a pointed fragment, whirling about to put his back to the wall. He even sidled along it for several feet toward the intercom before he realized that no physical weapon, no number of Cadre men would be of help now.

He dropped the chunk of wood and waited. Perhaps it would be too much for her. Perhaps . . .

"Wonderful! . . . That was wonderful!"

And she was there again, now standing close to Shaamlik with eyes more wondering wide and beautiful and dark than ever.

"You should have told me about this, my love. You should have told me!"

"You followed me." All he could think of was the immeasurably powerful and instinctive capacities of this . . . this monster child of the desert. She was less than half his age, without discipline, and just by following him she had learned to ride the time tracks with impunity in the time it takes for a stool to fall.

"You must teach me more! Please, my love!" She clasped her hands in front of her woman's breasts like a small girl pleading for a bedtime story. She seemed to have forgotten— like a recent spanking—that they had tried to kill each other.

"There is nothing more I can teach you, Cubus."

Her face puckered in disbelief. "But . . . that can't be! You can move in time!" She hesitated, looking at him with worshiping eyes. "Please . . . *Vitar*. You *are* a god. You can do *anything* you want. I will call you Vitar. Please teach me how to move *backward* in time. Please. I want to see my father."

As tears welled from her eyes and began to streak her cheeks, Tyrees was shaking his head. "If I could do that, Cubus, I would go back and see my own father."

"You won't teach me?" she sobbed, hanging her head.

Tyrees didn't know what to say or do. He couldn't predict the swings of her mind—he couldn't even follow them. And he was tired to the death.

"I told you. I can teach you nothing. Nothing."

She fell to her knees, hands still clasped fervently, eyes still blinking abject tears. "I haven't done anything wrong, have I? *Tell* me if I've done anything wrong!"

"You . . . haven't done anything wrong, Cubus."

"Then why—" Abruptly she stopped pleading and her head turned to take in the bed; then her smeared face broke into a radiant smile.

"I know!" she cried, leaping to her feet. "I will help your friend!"

Tyrees started. Shaamlik . . . "No, Cubus—"

"I will, I will!" Full of excitement, she pushed her hands under Shaamlik's skull. Tyrees came to the bed quickly and reached for them.

"No!"

He stopped. The single word was a snarl. Her face was distorted into the expression of a trapped jungle cat. When he took a step backward, it softened, so he continued to back away until he felt the wall.

"I will help her," she said, now calm again. She shook hair from her eyes and her chin lifted proudly, confidently. "You will see. You will see."

Dumbly, Tyrees nodded. She closed her eyes and lowered her head over Shaamlik. There had been no preparation of the kind he had always found necessary. There was no motion, no sound. He waited in the silence, watched in the semidarkness. Cubus's rich skin glowed softly along her cheek and the curve of an arm as she cradled the masked head. She was still naked to the waist—ripely voluptuous, alluring—and mad. Uncovered, Shaamlik was also naked, also beautiful in spite of the loss of flesh—and also mad.

He knew what Cubus was facing, though he did not know how. Unless her instinct came into play again, how could she possibly decide what had to be done? As powerful as her mind was, it was also unstable. It could be that she would end in scouring Shaamlik's mind like a dirty plate, as she had with one of her first victims.

He waited, not daring to approach, for a long time before the first sign came. It was only a tremor in Cubus's eyelids. He took a step forward before her eyes opened, unseeingly, and her face contorted with pain. She has seen the flames, he thought.

Staying where he was, he made the decision to follow them. Nothing seemed to matter much. Why not? He was preparing himself when Cubus's mouth opened. It would have been a hideous scream—had there been sound. Not even air escaped. She began to jerk back and forth convulsively—trying to remove her hands from beneath Shaamlik's skull? But it was as if they were joined, sisters sharing the same flesh and bone.

Tyrees was truly frightened. The silent scream, the spastic efforts to break free, went on and on. He was able to calm himself and was about to attempt contact when Cubus's head snapped back with such force that there was an audible crack—and she slid to the floor.

Tyrees moved to the bed slowly, trancelike, a man capable of no other speed, no other manner. Shaamlik had not changed. Her smooth mask still perfect; she breathed in the same slow, shallow rhythm, a feather moving in quiet air.

Slumped unnaturally on the floor, her head set rigidly at an odd angle, Cubus was a nightmare. Eyes wide and black, mouth wide and black, hands in the shape of claws. Horror had been slashed thickly onto her face with a heavy trowel.

Tyrees felt no triumph.

Twenty-six

Either everything matters or nothing matters. Choose to live or to die—it may be your only choice, after all.

—The Sayings of Meta-sol

"Is *CONDOR* BEING prepared?"

Tyrees's voice seemed small under the vast night sky, but there was no fear, no hesitation in it. Bolla sighed and leaned on the balcony rail, looking up at the cold, distant spits of light before answering. He shivered in spite of the warmth of the evening.

"Yes. She'll be ready in a few days. . . . I still don't know why you're doing this, Pol. I know you better than any man alive, and I still don't understand."

Tyrees's clothing made him difficult to see at the other end of the balcony, but he smiled now, and his teeth shone in the darkness. "It's just an exploration trip, Hans. I told you—I'm going to have a look at that red pathway."

Bolla snorted. "Of course, 'the red pathway.' Sounds like a quote—some symbolic nonsense from the bloody *Teraac*."

"Don't be sacrilegious, Doctor," said Tyrees with mock solemnity. "You know it's real. I've seen it."

"Oh, certainly." Bolla's voice was layered with weary

202

sarcasm. "A smear of red—what—light?—streaking off into infinity? How do you 'explore' *that?*"

"It is a pathway, Hans. Like the intergalactic pathways—only . . . different. And after all these years, I've only seen the one." It was Tyrees's turn to gaze upward.

"You're going to try to ride it."

A nod.

"For God's sake, *where?*"

A shrug. "Wherever."

Bolla sighed again, this time with resignation. Heaving his bulk from the balcony rail, he shuffled over to stand behind Tyrees. He spoke very mildly, but with sincerity—and not a little mirth.

"Look at what you leave behind you. You and Radis too—a retired professor, a fat old fart who'd rather spend his last days tinkering with dull statistics than play at being king of the hill. I'll make a mess of it, Pol."

"No, you won't."

"You and Radis—you're both abandoning me."

Tyrees chuckled. "We're just quicker on our feet, Hans. Now you have to hold the bag."

"Humph. Will Radis ever become a Seer, Pol?"

"I don't know . . . probably not."

"Humph. Did you tell *him* that?"

"No. He didn't want to hear it, and it wouldn't have made any difference anyway."

They returned to silence for a time, but there was a strange communion in it. In a way, they listened for each other's thoughts, and each—an old man and one no longer young—believed he heard something similar. Finally growing edgy, Bolla took out his handkerchief and blew his nose loudly.

"You know, Pol, if you stay away too long . . . I won't be here when you get back."

Tyrees turned to him. The now dull flame in the blue eyes flared for a moment. He knew that Bolla had even less time than his friend suspected because more than old age had begun to feed on the corpulent body. But he was not going to watch another father die.

"You'll be here," was all he said as he turned back to the rail to stare into the darkness.

"And the New Covenant? Who's going to look after the store while you're gone?"

"It can look after itself now, Hans. If it can't, it doesn't deserve to survive."

Bolla was disconcerted by this new stoicism. "Oh my! My my my! Such a cavalier attitude from their Vitar. . . . Could it be—could it just be that their young god knows that he will become even more of a god if he's absent?"

Though Bolla couldn't see it, Tyrees smiled mirthlessly. "You're playing the psychologist again, *Doctor*. You're needling me again."

"Needling? Of course not. I'm just trying to understand you. Ambition is a wonderful thing, after all . . . But the *godhead?*"

Now Tyrees laughed outright. It was a harsh sound, crashing into the night. Bolla waited with growing anxiety for his response.

"Perhaps you're right. . . . But I've discovered that the job isn't all it's stacked up to be. I'm all out of miracles."

"Humph . . . Tell me, is Shaamlik going with you?"

"Yes," he said.

There had been a shade of hesitation that Bolla didn't miss. Something stirred in the pit of his stomach. His vision blurred. He frowned and put his hand on the back hunched in front of him. All he could see was the skin crinkling beneath the gleaming skull as Tyrees looked up at the stars.

"You have no intention of coming back, do you?"